Tales of Nasreddin

Tales of Nasreddin
181 Mulla Nasreddin Stories

translated by
Henry D. Barnham, C.M.G.

with a foreword by
Sir Valentine Chirol

IBEX Publishers
Bethesda, Maryland

Tales of Nasreddin. 181 Mulla Nasreddin Stories
Translated from the Turkish by Henry D. Barnham
Foreword by Sir Valentine Chirol
Originally published in 1923

new material copyright © 2006 Ibex Publishers, Inc.

All rights reserved. No part of this book may be reproduced or
retransmitted in any manner whatsoever except in the form of a review,
without permission from the publisher.

Manufactured in the United States of America

The paper used in this book meets the minimum requirements of the
American National Standard for Information Services – Permanence of
Paper for Printed Library Materials, ANSI Z39.48-1984

Ibex Publishers, Inc.
Post Office Box 30087
Bethesda, Maryland 20824
Telephone: 301-718-8188
Facsimile: 301-907-8707
www.ibexpublishers.com

Library of Congress Cataloging-in-Publication Information

Tales of Nasr-ed-Din Khoja.   Tales of Nasreddin Khoja : 181 Mulla
Nasreddin stories   /   translated by Henry D. Barnham, with a foreword
by Valentine Chirol.
p. cm.
ISBN 0-936347-69-4 (alk. paper)
1. Nasreddin Hoca (Anecdotes)   I. Barnham, Henry D. (Henry Dudley),
b. 1854.   II. Title
PN6231.N27 T3 1999
398.2'09561—21   98-042587
                                                                      CIP

FOREWORD

AT a time when some profess to believe that a "new" Turkey is emerging from the welter of war and massacre and ruin in the Near East, my friend Mr. H. D. Barnham, C.M.G., whom I first met more than forty years ago at Constantinople on the threshold of his long career in the Levant Consular Service, has, not inopportunely, produced an English replica of the homely picture of the Turk by a Turk which still enjoys, in the quaint tales of Nasr-ed-Din Khoja, an absolutely unique popularity in Turkey itself.

It is not of course a picture of the ruling Turk, black-coated with a Western veneer, as he learnt to posture at the Porte and at Yeldiz Kiosk or more recently at Angora and at Lausanne, but of the primitive and much more picturesque Turk — simple-minded and blissfully ignorant, patient and plodding, gifted with a broad sense of humour,

FOREWORD

and by nature good-tempered and easy-going, but a born fighter and apt to " see red " when his racial and religious passions are unloosed " by superior order "—as he lived and moved and had his being five centuries ago, and still continues to do, in his "ancient and renowned homelands of Asia Minor."

The Turks have never wielded the pen as effectively as the sword, and Turkish literature, like the polite language of the Stamboul *literati* and of the Ottoman bureaucracy, has been largely borrowed from or modelled upon Persian and Arabic, under the influence of the higher civilisations with which a rude race of invaders from the wilds of Central Asia first came into contact. Nasr-ed-Din Khoja, on the contrary, speaks the simple, unsophisticated tongue of the Turkish people. The tales originated about five hundred years ago, and they have passed chiefly by word of mouth from generation to generation; but their actuality is still such that only twenty years ago they were tabooed by the Sultan Abdul Hamid, who scented danger to his Imperial authority in the Khoja's frequent jibes at those who in his day stood for authority, and especially for judicial authority. The "Young Turks" raised the taboo after the Revolution of 1908, but perhaps if the Khoja's ghost could have visited the other day the Conference Hall on the Lake of Geneva, it might yet have been heard chuckling over Ismet Pasha's lofty indignation that anybody should venture to question the unimpeachable methods of Turkish justice.

Patronymics being rarely used in Turkey, Nasr-ed-Din, or "Victory of the Faith," was the name given by his parents to the author of the tales, and Khoja, meaning "Master" or "Teacher," is the honorific title which he subsequently acquired. He was born probably after the middle of the fourteenth century and was a native of Sivrihissar in the district of Angora which has lately leapt into fame. He was sent at an early age to be taught the essentials of Mohammedan religious and legal learning according to the Hanafiya school at Konia. He qualified thus to be a schoolmaster and an "Imam," or leader of public prayers in the Mosque, and he also became a Cadi, or magistrate dispensing Mohammedan Canon

FOREWORD

Law, which was in theory the only law of the land, tempered though it might be frequently by weightier considerations of a material order. He belonged to what might perhaps be called the middle classes, if such a designation were not somewhat inappropriate to the Turkish social structure.

He grew up when the Turkish conquerors were rapidly building a vast Empire on the ruins of earlier Mohammedan states in Western Asia as well as of Christian kingdoms and principalities in South-eastern Europe. They had not yet captured Constantinople, where the shadow of the old Byzantine Empire still survived, but they had encircled it. Suddenly in the year 1400 Sultan Bayazid, surnamed Yilderim, the "Thunderbolt," was arrested in the full tide of unbroken victory by the furious invasion of Timurlange, or Timur the Lame, a descendant of the great Jenghiz Khan. His Tatar hordes poured forth from the old and then still overflowing Central Asian reservoir of hungry humanity, and he wielded a mightier thunderbolt than Bayazid's. The Turkish armies which had carried the Cres-

FOREWORD

cent to the banks of the Danube were outnumbered, out-generalled, overwhelmed, and routed with a great slaughter by Timur's hosts in the neighbourhood of Angora. But that was long before the dawn of Turkish "Nationalism," and Nasr-ed-Din Khoja appears to have had no scruple in transferring his allegiance to the victorious Timur, at whose Court he enjoyed great favour as a jester.

Timur, it must however be remembered, was as good a Mohammedan as Bayazid, and if he sometimes spent the morning building up pyramids of heads, cut off with equal impartiality from Bayazid's defeated Turks and from the Christian knights who fell in the defence of Smyrna, he always put in a punctual appearance at noonday prayers in the Mosque. It may, moreover, be doubted whether a change of masters had more than a passing effect upon the life of the people, who were accustomed in those days to the perpetual tramp of fierce competing armies, which finds indeed few echoes in Nasr-ed-Din Khoja's tales. Yet if he became a Court jester he never demeaned himself to abject flattery. When Timur on one occasion asked him to say what would become of him on the day of Judgment, he boldly replied that His Imperial Majesty should not worry or have the slightest doubt on the subject; for he would assuredly have a seat of honour where his forbears, Jenghiz Khan and Hulagu, had already gone—straight to Hell. That may well have been one of the tales that gave personal umbrage five hundred years later to Abdul Hamid!

For the most part, however, it is with the ordinary doings of humbler folk, with their oddities and weaknesses, with their household squabbles and social differences, with their farmyards and their animals, that the Khoja loves to deal in his own impish and seldom unkindly way. Like all real humorists, he is just as ready to laugh at himself as at others, and "Imam" though he was, even his religion often sits lightly upon him, for with his last breath he scandalises his wife by making fun of the grim angel of death, Azrail, whom he sees already hovering near him. He is, in fact, always intensely human, and for that reason not only is his tomb at Akshehir still a favourite place of popular pilgrimage for Turks from near and far, but his tales may well appeal to readers in all lands who can appreciate a human document.

VALENTINE CHIROL.

34 CARLYLE SQUARE, CHELSEA.
    1923.

TABLE OF CONTENTS

	PAGE
FOREWORD	5
INTRODUCTORY	21
THE INNKEEPER'S BILL	25
DOUBTING THE WISDOM OF PROVIDENCE	30
SEEING DOUBLE	32
TAMERLANE'S ELEPHANTS	33
THE THREE FRIARS	35
TEACHING TAMERLANE'S DONKEY TO READ	37
THE COOK AND THE BEGGAR	41
THE KHOJA AND THE BEAR	42
PUTTING THE BABY TO SLEEP	44
STRANGE DOMESTIC ECONOMY	46
SELLING WIND TO THE VILLAGERS	47
THE KHOJA'S HOROSCOPE	50
THE PRIZE TURKEY	51
ANSWER TO PRAYER	53
THE GALOSHES	54
THE KHOJA AND THE TAILOR	55
THE VILLAGE FAIR	56
THE KHOJA'S TACT IN MANAGING HIS WIVES	58
A DREAM ABOUT NINE GOLD LIRAS	58
DRINKING SEA-WATER	59
MARRIED OR SINGLE? OFF WITH HIS HEAD!	59
TRICKS OF THE SILK-TRADE	61

TABLE OF CONTENTS

	PAGE
THE KHOJA'S HOUSE ON FIRE	63
THE KHOJA'S FEIGNED ASSAULT UPON HIS WIFE	64
A WARRIOR'S RECORD	67
DISEASE CALLED "LOSS OF APPETITE"	69
THE "POISONED" DISH OF BAKLAWA	71
COUNTING THE DONKEYS	74
THE GOVERNOR'S WIFE	79
THE CLUMSY BARBER	81
THE KHOJA CAUGHT STEALING WHEAT AT THE MILL	81
THE KHOJA AS A MUSICIAN	82
THE "BASTINADO"—PUNISHMENT FOR DRUNKENNESS	83
THE KHOJA GOES HUNTING WITH TAMERLANE	85
THE KHOJA APPOINTED "JUDGE'S SHADOW"	86
SELLING PICKLES	90
A SUIT FOR PAYMENT OF "NOTHING"	90
THE KHOJA'S CONVICTION THAT HE WAS DEAD	91
DISPUTE IN COURT BETWEEN TWO LOW WOMEN	92
THE KHOJA DIRECTS HIS OWN FUNERAL	94
THE SCALDING SOUP	95
THE KHOJA'S PARABLE FOR YOUNG CHILDREN	96
AN IMPIOUS PETITION	98
A DISPUTATION ON PHYSICAL PHENOMENA	99
SETTING A LIGHT TO THE FURZE ON THE DONKEY'S BACK	107
CLIMBING A MOONBEAM	108
THE KHOJA AS A LETTER-WRITER	109
AN ASS'S COLT BORN WITHOUT A TAIL	109
SOCIAL AMENITIES—AN ACT OF DISCOURTESY	111
A STRANGE WAY OF RIDING A DONKEY	112
TAMERLANE IN HELL	112
THE KHOJA CANNOT READ PERSIAN SCRIPT	113
THE KHOJA AND THE JEW	114
SINGING IN THE TURKISH BATH	118

TABLE OF CONTENTS

	PAGE
THE SLEEPLESS, HUNGRY KHOJA	119
DAMAGES FOR THE LOSS OF A COW	120
THE KHOJA'S NIGHTCAP	121
WEEPING AT THE BEDSIDE OF HIS SICK WIFE	122
GARLIC AND HONEY	123
THE CAT AND THE MEAT	125
THE UNPAID GROCER'S BILL	126
BREAD AND SALT	127
THREE THOUSAND PIASTRES FOR A PAIR OF TONGS	128
CHEWING MASTIC GUM	130
THE KHOJA AND MULETEERS IN THE CEMETERY	130
THE KHOJA KICKED DOWNSTAIRS	132
THE KHOJA SCANDALIZES THE WEDDING PARTY	132
A DISH OF YOUGHOURT FOR TWO	134
THE KHOJA IS CAUGHT STEALING IN A GARDEN	135
HE PULLS THE MOON OUT OF THE WELL	136
THE QUAILS	136
THE IMPORTUNATE CREDITOR	137
TAMERLANE AND THE ACCOUNTS	139
THE NOBLEMAN AND THE KHOJA'S WIFE	140
THE ORDEAL	141
SELLING HIS TURBAN AT AUCTION	144
GIVES THANKS FOR THE LOSS OF HIS DONKEY	144
COUNTING THE DAYS OF RAMAZAN	145
THE LOAN OF A CAULDRON	146
TAMERLANE DISGUISED AS A DERVISH	147
GEESE AT AKSHEHIR HAVE ONLY ONE LEG	149
A WAGER: THE KHOJA'S VIGIL	151
A SAFE HIDING-PLACE FOR MONEY!	156
TAMERLANE'S TITLE	158
WHEN A MAN MARRIES HIS TROUBLES BEGIN	158
"RAIN COMES FROM GOD"	159

TABLE OF CONTENTS

	PAGE
ONE POMEGRANATE FOR EACH QUESTION ANSWERED	160
THE KHOJA AND HAMED GO WOLF-HUNTING	161
INSHALLAH (PLEASE GOD)	162
TAMERLANE'S DREAM	163
CONSCIENCE-MONEY	164
WHO SHALL FEED THE DONKEY?	164
QUESTION OF PRECEDENCE AT PUBLIC PRAYERS	167
TAMERLANE AND THE FIGS	170
THE HEART OF A TYRANT	172
"TO-MORROW MAY BE THE JUDGMENT DAY"	174
THE KHOJA'S HORSE IS "LEFT-FOOTED"	176
THE KHOJA TOSSED BY AN OX	176
AN EMBARRASSING QUESTION	177
HE MOURNS FOR HIS DONKEY—NOT FOR HIS WIFE	178
THE KHOJA SLAPS THE JUDGE IN COURT	179
MEASURING THE EARTH	180
A WAY TO MAKE THE DONKEY GO	180
THE KHOJA AND THE FOX	181
THE KHOJA IS CARRIED OFF TO THE MORTUARY	183
HE DREAMS THAT HE IS BEING FORCED TO MARRY AGAIN	185
MISTAKEN IDENTITY—A CONFUSION OF THOUGHT	186
THE KHOJA AS A LAD PERVERSE AND INTRACTABLE	186
THE LOST SADDLE-BAG	187
CARRYING THE BLIND MEN ACROSS THE RIVER	188
THE DATE-STONES	189
THE FEAST OF TANTALUS	189
SPECTACLES REQUIRED TO SEE A DREAM	192
HOW THE EARTH MAY "TURN TURTLE"	192
A RECIPE FOR COOKING LIVER	193
THE KHOJA'S MOTHER-IN-LAW DROWNED	194
THE VICIOUS DONKEY	194
CAN A MAN BITE HIS OWN EAR?	195

TABLE OF CONTENTS

	PAGE
DRIVING TO SIVRI-HISSAR IN HIS NIGHT-CLOTHES	196
THE GREENGROCER'S BILL	197
AMMONIA AS A STIMULANT	198
THE DRUNKEN CADI	199
YOUNG NASR-ED-DIN IN CHARGE OF THE STREET-DOOR	200
THE KHOJA MAKES GAME OF THE BLIND MEN	201
THE MIDNIGHT PATROL	202
THE BELLOWS	202
THE LOAN OF A DONKEY	203
THE HARE AND THE BARLEY-MEASURE	203
THE OMNIPRESENT DEITY	205
A SUMMARY OF MEDICAL SCIENCE	206
THE KHOJA CANNOT TELL WHICH IS HIS RIGHT SIDE IN THE DARK	206
THE KHOJA'S ABYSSINIAN PUPIL HAMED	206
THE CHANGELING	207
RIDDLES IN THE PULPIT	208
CHANGE FOR A POUND	209
THE KHOJA HIDES IN THE PANTRY	211
A PLOT TO STEAL THE KHOJA'S SHOES	211
TRAVELLERS' TALES	212
THE KHOJA AND THE STUDENTS	213
THE NATIONAL DISH "HELWA"	214
THE GAME OF "JEREET"	215
THE KHOJA AND THE SHEPHERD	216
BUYING FLUTES FOR THE VILLAGE BOYS	217
THE KHOJA AS A NIGHTINGALE	218
THE KHOJA AND THE BEGGAR	218
IMPERTINENT CRITICS	219
TAMERLANE AND THE KHOJA AT THE BATH	221
THE KHOJA TONGUE-TIED	221
THE FISH THAT SWALLOWED JONAH	222

TABLE OF CONTENTS

	PAGE
HONEY FOR THE CADI OF KONIA	223
A CURE FOR THE SCAB	224
THE DIRTY MELONS	225
INSTRUCTIONS TO THE DONKEY	226
THE KHOJA ILL-TREATS HIS DAUGHTER	227
THE BED-QUILT	227
THE KHOJA'S SKILL WITH THE BOW	229
PAYMENT FOR ATTENDANCE AT THE TURKISH BATH	230
GOD'S GUEST	231
HARE SOUP	232
THE KHOJA AND THE TROOPER	233
THE KHOJA AND THE VINEYARD	235
THE KHOJA AND THE SIEVE	236
THE DONKEY'S BARLEY RATION	237
THE KHOJA BUYS A SPORTING DOG FOR THE GOVERNOR	238
THE DONKEY AND THE FROGS	239
LOAN OF HIS DONKEY	240
LAYING EGGS AT THE TURKISH BATH	240
"GLOOMY FATIMA"	241
HE SHOOTS A FIGURE IN THE MOONLIGHT	242
THE PLEASURE PARTY	243
THE KHOJA'S WIFE PROVOKES A SCANDAL	244
CARRYING FOWLS TO SIVRI-HISSAR	246
RUSE TO OBTAIN AN INVITATION TO A WEDDING	246
VILLAGERS COMPLAIN OF THE KHOJA TO THE CADI	247
YOUNG NASR-ED-DIN STEALS THE MISER'S GOOSE	248
THE BOYS PADDLING IN THE RIVER	249
THE KHOJA ARRESTED FOR CARRYING ARMS	249
THE ROAST CHICKEN	250
WHERE TO STAND WHEN CARRYING THE COFFIN	251
THE KHOJA'S LAST INSTRUCTIONS TO HIS WIFE	251
THE APPARITION	252

THE KHOJA AND HIS DONKEY.

LIST OF ILLUSTRATIONS

THE KHOJA AND HIS DONKEY	*Frontispiece*
	FACING PAGE
THE KHOJA PRESUMES TO QUESTION THE WISDOM OF PROVIDENCE	30
THE KHOJA AND THE BEAR	42
THE KHOJA PERFORMS ON THE MANDOLINE	82
THE KHOJA IN THE CEMETERY	130
THE FLOOD	172
THE FEAST OF TANTALUS	190
THE KHOJA HIDES IN THE PANTRY	210

INTRODUCTORY

BOOKS upon Turkish folk lore have been written by the late Sir William Whittall, Mr. A. Ramsay and Mr. H. C. Luke. All have dwelt upon the personality of Nasr-ed-Din Khoja and quoted one or more of his better-known tales. As far back as 1855 some of them were translated by Camerloher into German and published at Trieste, and in 1884 there was published in English at Ipswich, but only in a form suitable for private circulation and in an edition limited to one hundred and fifty copies, a small collection entitled " The Turkish Jester, or the Pleasantries of Cogia Nasr Eddin Effendi," purporting to have been " translated from the Turkish by George Borrow." This is, therefore, the first English translation of the Tales as a whole published for the general public.

Twenty years ago there were probably not more than fifty tales in print in Turkish,

INTRODUCTORY

though very many more were well known to the Turkish people, and to such foreigners as lived in close contact with them. The enlarged edition used for the purpose of this volume was issued in Constantinople in 1909, and its editor stated in a postscript that he had devoted many years to collecting the tales, but that in view of the great difficulty of obtaining permission to publish them during the reign of Abdul Hamid he had laid them aside, waiting for better times. Directly after the Turkish Revolution and the proclamation of the new Constitution in 1908, he had made an appeal to the public for well authenticated versions of the tales, with the result that he had been able to collect altogether some 380 tales or short anecdotes. Many are followed in the Turkish edition by a footnote stating the authority on which they are given, and in some cases there are two or more versions of the same story. That there should be such discrepancies is natural where the stories have passed from mouth to mouth among an illiterate people. In the present work the translator has been obliged to reject a good many, some because they are uninteresting

INTRODUCTORY

and some because their crudity offends against good taste or their humour depends upon a play of words which may amuse those who know Turkish but loses all point in translation.

The illustrations are adapted from those of a Turkish artist named Khalid Effendi, which, although they may have little artistic merit, give a very faithful representation of Turkish features, costumes and surroundings.

In the flesh the Khoja lived five hundred years ago, but in his tales he still lives to-day as he did then amongst his people, who, as far as the vast majority are concerned, still live to-day in all essentials as they lived then. His memory is as green as ever, and his tomb is a favoured place of pilgrimage, albeit not for any odour of sanctity attaching to it. The Turks may have had many "saints," but they have only one "Khoja." In everything he did or said there was not only something impish and incongruous which provokes to laughter and promotes good fellowship, but also an enduring element of sanity and reality. His name indeed is a household word wherever the Turkish

INTRODUCTORY

language is spoken. Sober, beturbaned citizens in the local coffee-shops which are their clubs, travellers at a lonely khan resting from their long caravan journey, and brigands on the mountain side carousing round a log fire, take equal delight in telling and re-telling these tales, and, as they do so, they look over their shoulders and search the shadows with an eerie feeling that the old gentleman is somewhere near—lurking, listening, laughing.

Although this English version must lack the infinite charm of the Turkish text, the translator hopes that the reader will find these tales not uninteresting. Returning home perhaps rather weary of mind after his long day's work, let him find his slippers, and perchance his pipe, then seek his comfortable arm-chair, and take up the " Khoja."

TALES OF NASR-ED-DIN KHOJA

The Innkeeper's Bill

A MERCHANT was travelling to another country and put up at a Caravanserai on the road.

The landlord gave him for supper a fowl, two eggs, and half a loaf of bread, and a feed of hay for his horse.

Early next morning before starting he called the landlord and said, "We will settle the bill when I come back."

He left, and when he returned three months later he put up at the same place, when the landlord served him as before with a fowl and two eggs, and gave his horse a feed of hay. Next morning as he was leaving he called for the bill. The landlord answered, "I am afraid it will be rather stiff, but so long as you are not particular about a trifle we shall easily come to terms. Come now! Allowing a discount of one hundred piastres

—I think two hundred would be about right. But mind! only on condition that you put up here whenever you pass this way."

The merchant, who knew very well the value of money and what is a fair profit was scandalized, and cried, "What do you mean by charging two hundred piastres for two fowls, four eggs, and bread? Have you taken leave of your senses, or are you trying to cheat me?"

The landlord answered, "I told you the bill would be rather stiff, but let me go over the items. I will make it as plain as a pikestaff—then you will see that you have no right to accuse me of extortion or trying to cheat you.

"Let us suppose that the fowl which you ate three months ago had laid an egg every day—that would make more than ninety eggs. If they had been put to hatch there would have been as many chickens, and these of course would grow up and lay as many eggs. Let us add to these what you have now eaten on your return journey.

"Now let us suppose that three years pass. I should have a large poultry yard—all from your fowls and eggs—and you can easily

THE INNKEEPER'S BILL

calculate that I would have made hundreds and hundreds of piastres out of them. I have allowed you a big discount and am content to take only two hundred piastres, which at this rate does not represent the capital which I have lost."

The claim was of course disputed and the case came into Court.

The landlord sent word beforehand to the Cadi that he had received a very fine fat goose and hoped he would do him the honour of joining him at dinner.

When the case came on for hearing the Judge turned to the merchant, and asked, " Did you make any bargain with the landlord before you ate his fowls and eggs ? "

" As I intended to call again on my way back, I did not think it necessary to bargain about such trifles," he answered.

" Did you make any agreement for your board when you came back ? "

" I did not."

" Did you say how long you would be before you came back ? "

" No, I did not."

" During an indefinite period is it not possible to rear thousands of eggs and thousands of chickens from two fowls and four eggs ? Your answer, please, yes or no ? "

" Yes, certainly," said the merchant; but though he made certain reservations, they were not allowed and judgment was given against him for the two hundred piastres.

Just at that moment he felt somebody touch his skirts and turned to see a poor man, who told him that Nasr-ed-din Khoja could get him out of his difficulty. So he ran off at once and told him all about it, whereupon the Khoja applied for the usual three days' stay of execution with a view to appealing against the judgment.

On the third day the Khoja did not put in an appearance.

The court waited for an hour and then the constable was sent to his house to bring him.

The Judge was naturally angry at the delay and asked him indignantly why he had not come in time and had kept the court waiting.

The Khoja answered quite coolly, " Don't excite yourself. I was just coming when my partner at the farm came in. I had sent for him because I heard that he was going

THE INNKEEPER'S BILL

to sow the fields with ordinary wheat. I at once went into the barn where I kept some wheat which I had boiled and kept ready for making bulghur * and filled the sacks with sufficient for the purpose.

"What was I to do? If I had not acted promptly the fellow would have sown the fields with wheat—ordinary wheat, mind you —which could not possibly give a good crop. Half of it we keep on joint account, a large part of it goes to buy the best seed, the rest is paid as tithe. Think of it! My only hope would have been gone! I said to myself, 'Would it not be better to eat less bulghur in the winter and make sure of a good crop next year?' So I gave the man about two sacksful of the bulghur to sow it.

"That is why I am late, your Honour."

The Judge then addressed the Court, and as he did so, gave a scathing glance at those who thought the landlord had a bad case.

"Gentlemen," said he, "you have heard him. This man actually sows his fields with cooked wheat! Did you ever hear the like?

* *Bulghur.* Wheat, parboiled, dried in the sun, scaled, crushed, and re-boiled. It is the staple food of the villagers.

Is it possible for this Court to listen to people who talk such nonsense ? "

" Well, then," answered the Khoja, " is it possible to raise a large poultry-yard from roast fowls and boiled eggs, as you pretend, seeing that you condemn this worthy Moslem to pay two hundred piastres just for two fowls and four eggs ? "

The Judge found he had not a word to say, and the sentence was annulled.

Doubting the Wisdom of Providence

ONE hot summer day the Khoja was riding out to the village and stopped to rest under a big walnut tree.

He got down from his donkey, fastened the reins to one of the branches, and then lay down in the shade on the far side of the tree. He took off his turban, opened his vest, and set to work to make himself cool and dry the perspiration.

He noticed that there were some enormous pumpkins growing in the field close by, and then looking up, saw the walnuts on the tree.

THE KHOJA PRESUMES TO QUESTION THE WISDOM OF PROVIDENCE

DOUBTING THE WISDOM OF PROVIDENCE

" Lord God ! " he cried, " Thou has made both of these : tiny walnuts and pumpkins big as a calf—walnuts so very small compared with the size of the tree—a tree so large that two men cannot get their arms round the trunk, whose branches tower to the heavens and spread out like a tent for a quarter of an acre ! One would have thought it would have been better for those big pumpkins to grow on the walnut tree and the walnuts on the pumpkin plants ! "

Just then a crow was pecking at a walnut and struggling to get at the inside, when the nut broke off, and as it fell, hit the Khoja right on the forehead. It made him see stars, and he gave a cry of pain as he held his head in his two hands. Then he looked for his turban and jammed it on his head.

Anon a feeling of awe came over him, the fear of God entered his heart, and he cried, " Lord ! I have sinned. I repent. Never again will I presume to question the wisdom of Thy Providence. Thou movest in a mysterious way ! Ah ! what a mercy that pumpkins did not grow on the tree instead of walnuts, for my bald head would have been like broken ice ! "

TALES OF NASR-ED-DIN KHOJA

Seeing Double

THE neighbours persuaded the Khoja to fall in love with and marry a woman who had a squint. "Oh," said they, "she has such roguish eyes—fascinating beyond description."

One evening the Khoja bought a dish of cream and brought it in for supper.

"Is anybody else coming?" asked his wife. "One dish of cream would have been quite enough for us two, but two dishes are extravagant."

"Oh," said the Khoja, laughing, "in our house it is not at all a bad thing to see things double, that is, when they are articles of food."

They laughed and were just beginning to eat when the Khoja's wife said, "Excuse me, Khoja, but you make a great mistake if you think I am a woman who has no sense of self-respect. Who is that man there—that Khoja who is sitting next you?"

"Damn it!" said the Khoja, "you may see anything double in this house you may wish, but you have only one husband!"

Tamerlane's Elephants

IT is well known that there were elephants in Tamerlane's* army and that he made great use of them during the battle of Angora.

One of these elephants was sent to the Khoja's village for pasture. It made a clean sweep of all the crops and left absolutely nothing.

The villagers rebelled and, putting the Khoja at their head, went off to complain to Tamerlane. But they had such a dread of the tyrant that as they went along they began to sneak away, one by one and two by two, so that when the Khoja entered the presence of Tamerlane he noticed that they had all gone.

"Cowards!" said he to himself. "I'll pay you out for this!" and went straight in.

Tamerlane asked him the object of his visit, and he replied: "The people of my village beg to tender their grateful thanks to your Majesty for having deigned to send one of your elephants to them for pasture.

"But the poor beast wearies us with its

* See Appendix.

cries. It feels lonely in this strange land without a mate to keep it company. The villagers came with me into town, but, not daring to venture into your presence, they are waiting for me in the hope that I may bring them good news We are always your Majesty's most devoted, humble servants."

Tamerlane was highly pleased, and presented the Khoja with a robe of honour and other presents and every assurance of his Royal favour. As for the villagers, he only sent them his salaams. He immediately issued an Imperial Iradé commanding that a female elephant also should be sent at once to the village.

When the Khoja heard this he went off highly delighted not only at having got out of a scrape, but because of the handsome way he had been treated by Tamerlane. He arrived in the best of spirits and at once called the villagers together.

They cried: "Oh! Khoja dear, how did you get on? Give us some good news, please!"

The Khoja, with all the pride of a successful Ambassador, cried, "Good news! A female elephant is coming too."

THE THREE FRIARS

The Three Friars

CONTEMPORARY with Nasr-ed-din Khoja were three Friars who travelled with the object of entering into friendly discussion with the learned wherever they went.

When they came to Anatolia and made known their desire to meet the learned of that country, the people of Akshehir, just because they wanted to get some fun out of it, recommended to them Nasr-ed-din Khoja, and told them that he was always ready with an answer and that his conversation was delightful.

They decided to give a public dinner on the Palace Square and invited the Khoja and the Friars. When the postman arrived with the letter of invitation, the Khoja at once got on to his donkey with his stick in his hand and arrived at the place of meeting at the appointed time.

After the exchange of greetings and the usual prayer had been offered up for the preservation of the Padischah, they entered into conversation and explained to the Khoja what the Friars wanted.

"Well," said the Khoja, "I think it would be better that I should answer their questions first and afterwards we will enjoy ourselves. What can I do for you, ye Friars? Let me hear what it is you wish to ask."

The first Friar said, "Sir! Can you tell me where is the centre of the earth?"

The Khoja pointed with his stick to the fore-foot of his donkey on the off side. "There it is," said he, "just where my donkey is treading."

"How can you know that?" cried the Friars.

"Well, if you don't believe me, measure!" said the Khoja. "If it turns out to be an inch too little or too much, then you will have a right to talk."

The Friar did not know what to say and drew back.

Another Friar came forward and asked, "How many stars are there in the sky?"

"Exactly the same number as there are hairs on my donkey," said the Khoja.

"How can you tell that?" asked the Friars.

"If you don't believe me, count," said the Khoja. "If they are found to be one

THE THREE FRIARS

too many or one short, then you will have the right to find fault."

"Is it possible to count the hairs on a donkey?" they asked.

"Is it possible to count the stars in the sky?" answered he, at which the second Friar felt that he had nothing to say, and stepped aside.

Then the third Friar came forward and said, "Well, Khoja, tell me how many hairs there are in my beard?"

Without the slightest hesitation the Khoja replied, "Exactly the number of hairs there are in my donkey's tail."

"How can you prove it?" asked they.

"Quite easy!" said he. "We will pull out one hair from your beard and one from the donkey's tail, and if at the end they don't tally, well, then you will be right and I will be wrong!"

Teaching Tamerlane's Donkey to Read

SOMEONE presented Tamerlane with a beautiful big donkey. He was delighted, and his courtiers each had something flattering to say about it. They had "never seen its equal"; they thought it quite a "remarkable animal," and so on.

When the Khoja was asked what he thought of it, he answered, "A beautiful animal, indeed, and endowed, I believe, with a special gift. I think it may be possible to teach it to read."

"If," said Tamerlane, "you can teach it such an art, I will reward you handsomely; but if you fail, I will not only show you to be the fool you are, but I will punish you severely. Remember what the Persian poet Sadi says in the Gulistan.* He says that a funny man took it into his head to teach a donkey to speak, and that a sage heard of it and said, 'You cannot teach dumb animals to talk, but if you are a man, you may well learn from them to hold your tongue.'"

The Khoja replied, "May it please your Majesty, my proposal may seem foolish, but I am not so silly as to risk my life by offending you, nor am I quite mad. Be sure that I know what I am about. Give me three months to do it and some money for my expenses and leave the rest to me."

* *Gulistan* (Garden of Roses). A poem by the Persian Sadi of Shiraz.

TEACHING TAMERLANE'S DONKEY TO READ

All the Khoja's demands were at once granted, for, said Tamerlane, "Something funny is sure to come of it."

For three months the Khoja had a good time eating and drinking, and every morning and evening he gave the donkey his lesson.

When the time was up he arranged a meeting at a convenient place, and at the appointed day and hour walked in, leading the donkey, which was splendidly caparisoned with a gold-embroidered saddle. As he did so he bowed to the right and left, and took the donkey straight up to a book which had been placed on a stool in front. The donkey at once began to turn the pages over rapidly with his tongue, but when he came to a certain page he stopped, looking at the Khoja reproachfully, and began to bray loudly. At this the spectators looked at each other in amazement and burst out laughing.

Tamerlane was intensely amused; he gave the Khoja a handsome present and asked him how he had managed to teach the donkey.

This was his explanation:

"I took the donkey to my stable, then went out to the market and bought a hundred strips of parchment, which I took to the binder, who made them up into a big book.

" Then between each leaf I put a little barley.

" I spent the first five to ten days teaching him how to turn the pages, and as he turned them he would eat up the barley.

" After the first fortnight I would keep him hungry and then show him the book. I would open the first two or three pages, but he was so hungry that he shoved me on one side and began to turn them himself. Because he is a donkey he sometimes couldn't manage it.

" When he was hungry he would turn the pages quite well, but if he found that I had put no barley he would stop and begin to bray.

" I thought it was an excellent way of teaching him, and had many a good laugh over it in the stable.

" It amused me specially to think that I had found a way of getting a lot of money out of you and could eat and drink to my heart's content.

" The exhibition which the donkey has just given is the result of his having been kept on half-rations for two days.

TEACHING TAMERLANE'S DONKEY TO READ

"You saw how he crumpled up the pages, how reproachfully he looked at me and brayed.

"The book on the table is a beautiful manuscript specially used for the occasion, but the one in the stable has, of course, no writing in it at all, though it resembles this one from the outside.

"It has only scrawls and scratches to look like handwriting."

The Cook and the Beggar

A POOR man at Akshehir found a crust of dry bread and was thinking how he could find something to give it a relish when he passed by a cook's shop and saw a saucepan of meat fizzling and boiling on the fire. It gave out a delicious odour.

He went up to the saucepan and began breaking off little bits of bread, holding them in the steam until they became quite soft, and then he ate them.

The Cook looked on with astonishment at this very odd way of making a meal, and for some time said nothing, but no sooner had the poor man finished, than he caught hold of him and demanded payment.

The man protested that he had really had nothing from the Cook, and refused.

It happened that our Khoja was Cadi* of Akshehir at the time, and when the Cook brought the man before him he heard the charge in the ordinary course. Taking two coins from his pocket, he said to him, "Now listen to this," and he began to shake the coins and make them rattle. "All the satisfaction you get will be the sound of these coins."

The Cook cried out in amazement, "But, your Honour, what a way to treat me!"

"No!" said the Khoja. "It is a perfectly just settlement of the claim. A man who is so mean as to ask for payment for the steam of his meat will get the sound of these coins and nothing more."

The Khoja and the Bear

THE Khoja was cutting wood on the mountain when he saw an enormous bear come straight towards him. He at once climbed up a big tree a wild pear tree and the bear came and lay down underneath.

* Judge.

THE KHOJA AND THE BEAR.

THE KHOJA AND THE BEAR

The Khoja waited ever so long, but the beast did not stir. Evening came on, and as there was a bright moonlight he was able to see every movement of the bear from the tree.

At last the brute climbed up and began to eat the pears. Of course the higher he climbed the unhappy Khoja climbed higher still, until he had reached the topmost branch. The bear had now reached the one just below him. Then the Khoja quite lost his head and trembled like an aspen as he thought of the fearful death awaiting him.

Meantime the bear was hard at work pulling and eating the pears in the full light of the moon. Once he stretched out his paw until it almost touched the mouth of the terrified Khoja, who, under the impression that he was offering him a pear to eat, gave a loud scream and cried, "Thank you. Thank you. I don't eat pears."

The bear, who was still busy eating, could not imagine what had happened. He was so startled that he slipped and fell, carrying with him enormous branches and torn by thorns, until with a loud crash he came to the ground and lay there senseless.

In the morning the Khoja began to feel his way down the tree, thinking that the bear was dead, and when he had made sure, he jumped to the ground.

Now came the reward for the awful night he had spent. He stripped the bear of its big furry coat and proudly marched with it through the most crowded parts of the town, amid the cheers of the people, chuckling to himself the while.

Putting the Baby to Sleep

ONE evening his wife said to him, " I cannot think what has come to this child. It will keep on crying. I cannot do anything with it, and am at my wits' end.

" I wonder whether you could give it a charm to put it to sleep or read over it the prayer of the Seven Sleepers.* Do what you can! My poor arms ache with tossing it, and if it goes on much longer I shall drop down in a faint."

" Come now, don't worry," said the Khoja. " I think I know how to stop it. Take this book, open it, hold it up before

* See Appendix.

PUTTING THE BABY TO SLEEP

the child's face, and every now and then turn over the leaves gently."

But when he handed her the book she turned upon him in a fury. "Upon my word! I believe you would laugh at me, even if I were dying! Far better for you that I should die; then you can take a fresh wife and see what you can do with her! Think of it! For thirty years I have made my hair a mop to wipe your floor and worked for you like a slave! No!" she cried indignantly, "you can't go on playing the fool for ever!"

'Now, my dear," said the Khoja, "do be reasonable! If my advice is worth anything at all, you will do what I tell you. If not, why do you ask my help and trouble me for nothing?"

His wife now began to get calmer, but still she answered him resentfully, "Very good, but what is the book? What is it about?"

"Come, now, that is better," said the Khoja. "I will first tell you why I use it and afterwards you can say what you like.

"This book is known as the 'Koudouri.' When I am at the Mosque and give lessons from it, the Mollahs * all go to sleep, some of them even snore and talk in their sleep.

" Naturally, if this book has such a magical effect upon grown-up people, its effect upon a tiny little child will be like opium."

His wife saw that she had better do what he told her, and it is a fact that, thanks to the Khoja's happy inspiration, the child went off to sleep at once.

Strange Domestic Economy

THE Khoja took his donkey to the market and handed it over to the broker for sale.

The man proceeded to walk it round and cry, " For sale. A fine donkey—free action—so steady that you can drink coffee while riding him—soft mouth—young—coat in excellent condition."

The people all began to bid, and the Khoja, who had been standing by listening to the broker, said to himself, " If my donkey is such a fine animal, why shouldn't I buy it myself ? "

He at once began to bid eagerly and pushed up the price until it was knocked down to

* *Mollahs.* Theological students.

STRANGE DOMESTIC ECONOMY

himself. He then paid the full price to the broker and took the donkey away.

In the evening he was telling his wife what he had done, when she said, "A funny thing also happened to me to-day. The man with the cream was passing the door and I called him. He was weighing out the cream, and as I wanted to get more out of him I took my bracelet when he was not looking and put it among the weights. Then I caught hold of the cream and cleared out of the way."

When she said this the Khoja cried out, "Bravo! That is the way to do the housekeeping. I keep a sharp look-out in the market and you here at home!"

Selling Wind to the Villagers

ONE of the most remarkable things the Khoja ever did was to sell wind to the villagers.

One year he was appointed Imam* at a certain village during the Fast of Ramazan.* When the fast was over, the villagers refused to pay him the amount of wheat which was

* See Appendix.

TALES OF NASR-ED-DIN KHOJA

due to him for his services, on the ground that they had had a bad harvest.

The Khoja was very angry and said, "Very good! It is now the time to winnow the corn, but I will not let you have any wind. Get it if you can."

He then went up on to the top of a hill facing their threshing-floors and stretched a mat out on poles, to serve as a screen.

It is a fact that for several days not a breath of wind blew upon the floors and the villagers were alarmed to see that heavy clouds had collected and threatened rain.

A superstitious villager came to the Khoja and said, "If you will give me some wind I will give you twice as much as the Imam received from me last year."

The Khoja immediately made a hole in the mat pointing straight at the man's threshing-floor, and directly he went down he found that there was a steady wind blowing.

He at once set to work winnowing the corn and soon had great stacks of it ready. In great glee he proceeded to fill his sacks with corn and straw, piled them on his cart and carried them to the house for storage.

When his neighbours saw it they ran down

SELLING WIND TO THE VILLAGERS

to their threshing-floors, but when they came near they found that there was not a breath of wind.

Then another man said, "It is of no use. You cannot do anything. Go to the Khoja and promise to pay him his due. You will have to buy your wind."

He himself, seeing that there was no help for it, went off to the Khoja and made terms. The Khoja at once opened a hole in the mat facing this man's threshing-floor, and he immediately got what he wanted. Then the villagers rushed in a body up the hill to buy their wind from the Khoja, promising to pay him everything he demanded.

But the Khoja said, "My men! if you think you are going to cajole me into doing this, and when you have got what you want, break your word, you will be sorry for it. God will sift your corn for you in a way you won't like!"

The villagers, however, had received a lesson; they were afraid of him and kept their promise faithfully.

He opened a hole in the mat directly opposite to each man's threshing-floor and they all had a good harvest. They paid the Khoja twice the amount due to him—enough wheat to live like a fighting cock for a whole year! He loaded it on the ox-carts, and then they all had dinner together at "Farewell Fountain," just outside the village. After the Khoja had said a prayer, he turned to the villagers and said, "You see that if God does not guard a man's rights by His mighty Hand, He does so by His wind!"

The Khoja's Horoscope

A FRIEND asked the Khoja under what star he was born.

He answered, "I remember that mother told me I was born under the sign of the Lamb."

"Nonsense!" said his friend. "The Lamb is not a constellation. You must mean the Ram."

"Well!" answered the Khoja, "it is forty years since mother cast my horoscope. Surely that is time enough for a lamb to grow into a ram!"

The Prize Turkey

ONE day the Khoja saw a bird about the size of a pigeon sold in the market for twelve pounds.

"Evidently," said he, "birds are fetching a high price. Now is the time! To-morrow I will bring that prime turkey of ours here for sale."

Next day he tucked the turkey under his arm, and the bird, proud of its coral necklace, puffed itself out and showed that it highly approved of being carried with such care.

The Khoja entered the market with the bird under his arm, and in full expectation of getting a high price for him began to call out, "A prize turkey for sale—reared on my own farmyard."

When, however, he found that the highest bid was only ten piastres, he lost his temper, and said to the brokers and dealers, "For Heaven's sake what is the meaning of this? Only yesterday I saw you with my very eyes sell a painted bird no bigger than a pigeon for twelve pounds. You were all keen after it. You all joined in the bidding. Of course that bird was painted, but look at this!

Look at the natural colouring of pearl and coral on its neck. Look at its plumage! See how it glows with reflected light when the sun falls upon it, and how it swells itself out and hisses when it is angry and opens its wings and tail, just like a tent. It has plenty of meat on it. It is as big as a lamb, and in the farmyard when it preens itself and struts like a peacock, I am never tired of looking at it.

"Unfortunately, I am obliged to sell it, or I certainly would not. As I was leaving home my wife and I felt so bad about parting with him. It was quite heart-breaking. When we sobbed out, 'Oh oh!' he tried to cheer us up by saying 'Gool! Gool!'"

This vehement harangue caused the people much amusement, but at last one of them said, "Now, Khoja, don't get so excited. You are not very careful what you say. For instance, that bird you talk about was not a common painted thing. It was that well-known bird the parrot, famous for a variety of natural colours."

The Khoja, who perceived that all his hopes of getting money for the turkey had flown to the winds, cried out in his vexation,

THE PRIZE TURKEY

" Oh, yes, indeed! A parrot! What of that? Isn't it a bird after all? Has it anything special about it?"

The other, who wanted to rub it into him, said, " The parrot has this advantage over your turkey, that it can talk very well."

At this the Khoja pointed to the turkey, which had closed its eyes with philosophic calm, and said, " Your bird may know how to talk, but mine is a devil to think."

Answer to Prayer

THE Khɔja went to Broussa about some important business.

He went from one department to another, but could not get the matter settled. At last a friend said to him, " If you say your prayers every morning for forty days kneeling by the Mihrab* of the big Mosque, you will be answered, and on the forty-first day the case will be settled."

* *Mihrab.* A niche in the centre of the wall of a mosque which marks the direction of Mecca. The Imam stands before it when leading the congregation.

The Khoja did this, but nothing came of it.

At last one morning he went into the little prayer-house adjoining the big Mosque and prayed earnestly. Then by the mercy of God his prayer was heard and his case settled. The Khoja went straight to the big Mosque by the main entrance and cried with a loud voice, " Shame on you! You could not manage to do what your baby Mosque has done!"

The Galoshes

SOME friends invited the Khoja to a wedding.

When he entered the house he noticed that there was no one in attendance to receive the guests and take charge of their galoshes. These were all mixed up, so that no one could tell " t'other from which." Fearing that his galoshes might get lost in the confusion, the Khoja took a handkerchief out of his pocket, wrapped them up in it, and put them into his pocket.

He entered the room and was offered a seat. The gentleman who was sitting next

THE GALOSHES

to him saw that the Khoja's pocket was bulging out and noticed the end of the handkerchief.

"I fancy, sir," said he, "that you must have some rare book in that pocket."

"Yes," replied the Khoja.

"What is it about, may I ask?"

"It is a book on political economy," said the Khoja.

The man, wishing to carry on the conversation, asked again, "Did you buy it from the bookshop?"

"No," replied the Khoja; "I bought it from the shoemaker."

The Khoja and the Tailor

NASR-ED-DIN KHOJA went to Broussa on business. He walked into the market and bought a pair of cloth trousers, told the shopman to wrap them up, and was proceeding to pay and carry off the parcel when it occurred to him that as his trousers were not very old, he would do better to buy a light coat instead.

He turned to the shopman and said, "I

had meant to buy these trousers, but have changed my mind. Give me a coat for fifteen piastres instead."

"Very good!" said the shopman, and taking out a coat which he thought would fit him, handed it to him. The Khoja took it and was walking out when the shopman said, "You have not paid for it, sir."

"What next?" said the Khoja. "I bought the coat and left the trousers in place of them."

"But you did not pay for the trousers," said the man.

The Khoja looked very much astonished and said, "Upon my word, you Broussa people are funny fellows! Why should I pay for trousers if I never bought them?"

The Village Fair

"LET us go to the fair and have some fun," said the boys.

It was the Bairam holiday, and they went to a field outside the town to have some games.

The Khoja stood there watching them with

THE VILLAGE FAIR

the greatest interest when a young fellow snatched his turban from his head and threw it among the players. As they passed it on from one to the other, the Khoja ran after it; but though he struggled hard to get it back, it was no use, he could not do it.

The boys had rare fun over it.

"Oh, stop that," he cried. "Give me back my turban and let me go." But they only jeered and laughed and made such a noise that no one thought of listening to him.

He saw it was of no use and that he might wait there for hours and never get it back. So, saying "Drat the boys," he got on to his donkey and left.

As he was going along a friend met him and asked where he had been and why he had nothing on his head.

"Where is your turban?" he asked.

"Oh, it is playing over there," said the Khoja. "It suddenly remembered the days when it was young, and went to play with the boys at the fair."

TALES OF NASR-ED-DIN KHOJA

The Khoja's Tact in Managing his Wives

THE Khoja had two wives. He gave each of them a blue shell as a keepsake, telling them not to let anyone see it. One day they came in together and asked him, "Which of us do you love best? Who is your favourite?"

"The one," he answered, "who has my blue shell."

Each of the women took comfort. Each one said in her heart "'Tis I he loves best," and looked with scornful pity upon the other.

Clever Khoja! That is the way he managed his wives!

Dream about Nine Gold Liras

ONE night the Khoja dreamt that a man gave him nine gold liras and that he began to haggle and said to him, "You might at least have made it ten."

At this point he woke up, and finding that there was nothing in his hand, shut his eyes tight and stretched his hand out, saying, "Very well. Bring them here. I'll take nine."

Drinking Sea-water

THE Khoja was seized with a great thirst while walking by the sea-shore and could not resist drinking some salt water. Far from quenching his thirst, his throat was badly burnt and he felt horribly sick.

A little farther on he came upon some fresh water and drank to his heart's content. Then he filled his cap and took it back to the shore.

"Ah!" he cried, "stop those foaming billows and cease your swagger! Water indeed! I'll show you what water should be! Try this," said he, as he threw the fresh water into the sea.

Married or Single? Off with his Head!

A CERTAIN tyrant had a wife who committed adultery. From that time he conceived a hatred for women, and it became his practice whenever he heard people speak of a man as "learned" to send for him and whisper a question in his ear. If he did not receive an answer to his liking, he immediately ordered the man's head to be cut off.

Not knowing anyone else who could put a stop to this terrible state of things, they persuaded the Khoja to see what he could do.

The tyrant made him sit by his side and whispered in his ear the words, " Are you married or single ? "

The Khoja replied, " At my time of life ? Not married ? What an idea ! "

" Ho ! ho ! " said the tyrant, " so you too are one of them. Off with his head ! "

The Khoja, who saw at once that he was in deadly peril, cried out, " Don't be in a hurry !

" Suppose you were to put the question another way. Ask me, for instance, if I divorced my wife and afterwards took her back, or whether she died and I married again, or whether having already one wife I took two or three more. In any case I would be wrong, but one never knows one's danger until it is too late. Perhaps you remember that famous proverb, ' A horse that slips will never break its neck.' "

The tyrant was so pleased with the Khoja's answer that he countermanded the order for his execution.

Tricks of the Silk Trade

THE Khoja went to the market to sell some silk which his wife had spun, and the merchants tried to get it from him for nothing. "It would be a good thing to pay you out for this," said he to himself.

He found a big camel's head in a dust-heap, took it home and wound the silk round it, making it into a very big ball.

He then went to the market and showed it to some other silk merchants. One of them offered a sum small as compared with the size of the parcel, but when the Khoja reflected that it would be a fair price for the silk if it were weighed separately, he agreed, and cried, "Cash down!"

The man, however, was suspicious when he found that so big a parcel was to be had for so low a figure, and asked whether the silk had all been spun at the Khoja's house, or where, and he added, "I hope there is nothing inside."

The Khoja turned to the man quite coolly and said, "Head of a camel!"

The customer, who evidently thought this merely an exclamation of impatience, felt reassured and paid down the money. The Khoja took it and cleared off some of his debts with it. Then the man who had bought the silk went to his shop and untied it. When he found the head he at once went off to find the Khoja.

"Is this a nice thing for you to have done? When I asked you if there was anything in the parcel, you answered, 'No!' You have cheated me," said he.

The Khoja only laughed and said, "Oh! If you would only take to heart this lesson I have given you. It would be worth a thousand times more than the few piastres you gain by cheating! In the first place, you made far more than you ought to have done out of my wife's silk, which she had been spinning until her eyes nearly dropped out of her head and which I had such trouble to get rid of.

"In the second place I did not tell you a lie. I actually told you what I had done when I said to you, 'Head of a camel!' You bought it with your eyes open. If I had acted differently, if I had insisted on getting a higher price, either the silk would have remained on my hands at a time when

TRICKS OF THE SILK TRADE

I am hard up and in need of money, or, if I had sold it to you at that price, my conscience would have pricked me and I would have gone home miserable.

"Men of learning and piety do not go out of their way to cheat people, nor, unless they are absolutely obliged, do as I have done. You think it the end of all things if you cannot do me out of a little money, but Nasr-ed-din Khoja is an honest man, always ready to pay his debts and justify the means he employs to sell his things."

The Khoja's House on Fire

A FIRE broke out at the Khoja's house and one of his neighbours ran to find him.

"Run, Khoja!" he cried, "your house is on fire. I knocked at the door as I was passing, but there was not a sound. There is evidently nobody at home."

The Khoja did not look at all alarmed.

"My dear fellow," said he, "my wife and I have so arranged our domestic affairs that I have nothing to worry me. I have to earn a living out of doors while she looks after the house. I am sorry to trouble you, but would you kindly let her know? This is not my concern."

The Khoja's feigned Assault on his Wife

BEHOLD the Khoja in a violent passion with a big stick in his hand rushing after his wife and shouting, "I have had enough of you! I'll give you a good thrashing and pay you for all the annoyance you have caused me these thirty years! Then go and complain to anyone you wish!"

His wife ran along screaming, "Help! Good people of Mohammed! This fellow has gone mad again. Save, oh, save me!"

There happened to be a wedding at a house close by, and the guests, hearing the cries, rushed out into the street and carried the Khoja's wife into the harem for safety. They then turned to the Khoja and begged him to be quiet, saying, "We all know how foolish women can be; but is this a nice thing for you to do?—for you are a man of culture and you would be the first to find fault with us if we were to do it."

While they were trying to pacify him,

THE KHOJA'S FEIGNED ASSAULT ON HIS WIFE

the owner of the house came forward and said, "My dear Khoja, let me profit by this unpleasant business to ask you a favour. Of course I was rude not to have invited you to our party. It was partly because it was for young people and I was afraid you might find it tiresome, but I am so delighted to have this opportunity. Please do us the honour of joining us for a while and let us hear what it was all about."

Though these words served to calm the Khoja to a certain extent, he was still growling with indignation when he entered the house.

As the wedding breakfast was ready, the guests took their places. The Khoja at once began to describe how the quarrel had arisen and kept them all in a roar of laughter.

Just then some baklawa* was brought in. The Khoja ate from the dish which was placed before him with the greatest relish, while he continued his description of the quarrel, and then wound up by saying, "Lucky woman! Lucky rascal! So she took refuge here, did she? If I could have got

* *Baklawa.* Light, flake-like pastry flavoured with honey.

hold of her I would have given her ear a twist like this," said he, twirling the dish of baklawa round towards himself, which made the people laugh again.

"Ha! ha!" they said, "you can't help joking even when you are angry!"

After trying a variety of delicacies, the guests left the table and coffee was served.

The Khoja then made a humorous speech to those present. He said, "Our good neighbour here gave a wedding party, but did not invite us. As I found out that he was going to have some nice things to eat and especially my favourite dish baklawa, my wife and I thought the matter over and we got up this little pantomime so as to get our share. As for my little wife, I am really very fond of her. God bless her! Would you mind sending someone into the harem to let her know that I am waiting? We must be off, but I hope you will go on enjoying yourselves."

He left them marvelling at this very ingenious trick he had played them.

A Warrior's Record

VERY near to the Khoja lived a gallant officer devoted to the profession of arms. The Khoja noticed that it was his habit when he came home in the evening to shoot three arrows, one from the ground-floor, another from the first, and the third from the second floor. This happened so often that it aroused the Khoja's curiosity and he asked the officer to tell him the reason.

"If you are so anxious to know, come with me," said he, and took the Khoja into the stable. There he showed him a powerful charger of peerless beauty.

"It was on this steed," said he, "that I placed myself at the head of my Spahis and by a flanking movement caused the defeat of the Crusaders at the battle of Nicopoli."

So saying he shot an arrow into the air and the Khoja cried, "Bravo!"

Then they went up to the first floor. Here he showed the Khoja an armoury full of weapons of matchless price.

"Some of these arms," said he, "my ancestors brought from Tartary. They wore them during the conquest of Roumelia, at the defeat of the Servians near Adrianople, during the conquest of Bulgaria and at the great battle of Kossova. There are others which I wore myself at the battle of Nicopoli while pursuing the Servians and some also which I captured from the Crusaders. They will be an heirloom in my family for ever. To me they are of greater value than the most precious things of this world."

In his pride and joy he shot another arrow into the air.

The Khoja had listened to these details with very great interest.

They then went up to the top floor.

The officer now called his wife, who at once covered her face and came into the room. He bade her kiss the Khoja's hand.

The Khoja learned that this lady (who was a fascinating creature with a face like the light of the moon) was related to Princess Maritza of Servia, one of the wives of Sultan Bayazid, and that when the officer brought the Princess to the Sultan this lady was in her suite.

Turning to the Khoja he said, " She took a fancy to me directly she saw me, but when she heard of my prowess on the battlefield she

A WARRIOR'S RECORD

fell violently in love. From that time she was always in tears, but would tell no one the cause of her grief until at last the Princess noticed it.

"The Sultan issued his Iradé* and I married her.

"Her learning, virtue, intelligence, and refinement are even greater than her beauty."

When with a heart full of love and pride he shot another arrow into the air, the Khoja could no longer contain himself and cried, "You have every right to be proud! Those arrows speed in a worthy flight, and I hope that in future, whenever you shoot them, you will send one up also as a salute from Nasr-ed-din Khoja."

Disease called "Loss of Appetite"

A TRAVELLER called at the Khoja's house and he entertained him. He laid the table, put out the bread, and then went to fetch the dinner. When he came back he noticed that the bread was all gone. Without a word he went out again for more

* *Iradé.* An Imperial decree.

bread, but when he returned this time he saw that the meat was all finished.

He took the empty dishes and ran off for more, but when he came back there was not a scrap of bread left.

So he went to and fro until there was no meat left in the saucepan, nor bread in the bread-pan, nor had he ever had time to bring them in together so as to wait and see the man eat.

He asked him where he was going and the object of his journey, and he answered, " I am afflicted with a complaint called ' loss of appetite.' I am going to Broussa to see the doctor and get some medicine and shall come back at once. I hope we may meet again in a month at the latest. I have taken quite a fancy to you. When I come back I should like to spend a month with you and see what this fine climate can do for me."

" Oh! I am very sorry," said the Khoja, " but as I intend to go to the country in a day or two I shall not have that pleasure. I will therefore wish you good-bye now," and so he managed to get rid of him.

The "Poisoned" Dish of Baklawa

IN view of the high character and learning of the Khoja, the notables of Akshehir were anxious that their boys should profit by his instruction and appointed him head master of the town school.

One of the notables whose boy attended the school examined him on the lessons he was preparing. The boy answered his questions so well that his father was highly delighted and, calling a servant, bade him take the Khoja a present of a tray of baklawa.

It came just when lessons were going on, and the Khoja wondered how he could prevent the boys getting hold of it. He himself had been called away suddenly to attend a funeral, so, as he could do nothing with it till he came back, he called up the head boys and said to them, "I am putting this tray on the shelf here. Be careful you don't touch it. I don't quite trust the man who sent it, for we were once on very bad terms. Most likely there is something poisonous in it, and if so, it is not a mere practical joke, but a crime he has committed. Mind, it is your own look-out; but if you all die of

TALES OF NASR-ED-DIN KHOJA

poison, I shall be held responsible, and you will cause me to be thrown into prison and rot there."

When the Khoja had gone, the head boy, who happened to be his nephew and knew that this was only humbug, took the tray down from the shelf, sent for his particular chums, and tried to persuade them to join him in eating it.

The boys cried, "No! It is poisoned. The Khoja said so. We won't touch it. We don't want to die."

"It is a trick, boys. Just see me eat it! Now you can't say anything after that," said he, as he took some.

"All right," said the others; "but what answer are we to give the Khoja?"

"You leave that to me," said he. "I have got an answer ready that will quiet him. Now then, let us polish off the baklawa."

Feeling more at ease, the boys at once set to work and made a clean sweep of it, shouting and laughing as they did so.

That rascal of a nephew must have made his plans ever since the baklawa arrived, for no sooner had they finished eating it than he ran into the Khoja's room, caught hold

THE "POISONED" DISH OF BAKLAWA

of a penknife on the inkstand and broke it. At that moment the Khoja came in, and seeing the penknife, asked angrily who had broken it.

The boys all pointed to his nephew as the culprit.

"What did you do this for?" he demanded. "Do you want me to break your bones for you?"

The boy pretended to cry and said, "My pen broke. I tried to mend it with your penknife and broke the knife. Then I said to myself, 'How ever can I look Uncle in the face? What answer can I give him? If he comes in now, he is sure to give me such a thrashing that he will break every bone in my body. It were far better to die than bear such torture,' said I. Then I began to think what was the best way to kill myself. I did not think it nice to throw myself down the well, because it would make it smell. Then I suddenly remembered the baklawa on the shelf which you told us was poisoned. I took down the tray, and first I repeated the words of our Creed, 'There is no God but God, and Mahomet is his prophet'; then I said good-bye to my schoolfellows and sent word to my father and sister and to my poor mother who had been angry with me. I begged them all to forgive me, and then saying 'Bismillah!'* I shut my eyes and swallowed the baklawa. I did not forget to clean up the tray with my fingers, but . . . I am sorry to say . . . such is my unhappy lot . . . I did not die . . . I could not die!"

The poor Khoja, though exasperated at the loss of his favourite dish and the breaking of the penknife, which had been a present from his father, could not help exclaiming, "My lad, I am amazed that at your age you should have thought of such a clever plan. I am always ready with an answer whatever I am asked, but you will soon be able to give me points. It is quite clear that this is hereditary in our family."

Counting the Donkeys

IN Anatolia, when the villagers send their wheat to be ground at the mill, each one loads his own donkey, while one of them takes charge of the lot.

This is a far better plan than that four or

* In the name of God.

COUNTING THE DONKEYS

five men should remain at the mill for days together, each awaiting his turn.

It happened that our Khoja was once bound for the mill, riding one donkey himself and driving before him eight others loaded with wheat.

Suddenly a doubt crossed his mind, and he thought he had better count the donkeys. He did so, and found there were only eight. He was very much put out, for eight men had handed their animals over to him and one for himself should make nine.

He pulled up, got down, went back a long distance to the bend of the road, and after looking to see if the donkey were hiding behind the trees, came back disconsolate.

Before he got up, however, he counted them again, and lo! there were nine!

"Thank God," he cried, "they are all right!"

But of course it was not long before his doubts revived.

He began to count again, and would you believe it, there were only eight! So down he jumped in a terrible state of mind, went a long way back, but found nothing, and returned in despair.

Then when he counted them again and found that there were nine, it nearly drove him crazy.

Being, moreover, very superstitious, he called to mind tales about fairies and sprites and the pranks which they play upon poor mortals in the pathless desert. His brain was in a whirl.

After repeating a number of prayers he got up again and went on his way.

But would the Devil leave him alone? Something—some terrible power which he could not resist urged him on and made him count them again. There were eight! He jumped down in a frenzy, stamping his feet and shouting out imprecations and prayers to exorcise the evil spirits. Suddenly he heard strange sounds which made him tremble.

He looked, and lo! all the donkeys had scattered and were busy cropping the grass. He had no strength left to take off their loads and threw himself down in the shade of a tree.

Just then a traveller came down the road and the Khoja, obsessed by his fear of the evil-spirits, shouted to him to come. It turned out that they were acquaintances.

COUNTING THE DONKEYS

When the man saw how exhausted the Khoja was, he asked him the reason and he told him everything—how the spirits, not content with molesting people in town, conspire to torment poor mortals in the pathless desert.

"Don't worry, Khoja," said the man; "it is all your fancy."

But the Khoja swore that though he had not actually seen them he had heard their voices.

At this the man began to feel some doubts himself, but continued his efforts to cheer up the Khoja, who at last said,

"Please stay with me a little while and then help me on to my donkey and see me on my way."

The man took compassion on him and they sat down to have something to eat. The Khoja was soon himself again. He became quite lively and began to crack jokes. Then they collected the donkeys and he mounted one of them, saying, "Come, let us count them once more."

When, however, he again found that there were only eight, he turned to the traveller almost in tears and said, "There you see! Only eight! Oh! what a time I have had with these donkeys!"

The man burst out laughing. "Khoja! Khoja!" he cried, "why don't you count your foster-brother—the donkey you are on now. All this bother because you never counted your own donkey along with your other foster-brothers!"

The Khoja thought a moment, then, clapping his hand to his forehead, he jumped off his donkey, rushed up to the traveller and embraced him.

The man, who thought the matter very trivial, was taken aback and protested; but the Khoja cried, "God bless you! You have made me a man again. You have restored my reason and given me life. If this riddle, which is so very simple, had remained unsolved, I should either have gone mad or had a heart attack and died."

When one comes to think of it, the solution of the most difficult enigmas dazzles the eye with no brighter light of conviction than if they had been the simplest and most obvious problems.

The Governor's Wife

THE Governor of Akshehir was tied to his wife's apron-strings. She interfered in the affairs of the Government and began even to appoint and dismiss the officials.

Some of the leading men in the town went to the Khoja and begged him to try to put a stop to it. He had an interview with the Governor, in which he mentioned so many instances of the lady's interference that he persuaded the Governor not to allow her such liberty in future.

When she found that she was losing her influence over her husband, she wanted to know who it was that had been the cause of her receiving this rebuff, and found out through the Khoja's wife that it was he.

It was the Khoja's custom every summer when he returned from the country to stay a few days at the Governor's house, and the lady took the opportunity to invite him to bring his wife with him.

One day while the Khoja and his wife were chatting together in his private room, the lady came in and began to tease the Khoja. Then she gave him some drink and made him tipsy. Now said she, "Let us have a game. There is a pack-saddle I saw lying out there by the wall. Bring it here."

The Khoja, who was beyond all power of resistance, went to fetch it. She persuaded him to let them put the saddle on his back. They then made something to serve as a bridle, and the lady mounted. The Khoja began to neigh like a horse, and while he was careering round the room with his charming rider, his wife called the Governor, telling him to look through the keyhole and see what was going on. As the Khoja galloped along, kicking and prancing, the Governor roared with laughter, but at last he felt he must go in, and opened the door.

"Fie! fie! Khoja!" he said. "What on earth are you doing?"

"Ha!" said the Khoja quite coolly, "now you see with your own eyes what she has done with me. It was because I wanted to protect you from this tyranny that I gave you that piece of advice. So far as we are concerned we are only individuals. The reins of Government are not in our hands. Our authority is purely domestic and restricted to looking after our own wives at home.

THE GOVERNOR'S WIFE

It does not matter what people say of us, because it does not affect others; but if you, the Governor, put the bridle into your wife's hand like this, the whole country suffers."

The Governor was doubly impressed by this piece of advice, and as to his wife, she gave up the struggle and retired in disgust.

The Clumsy Barber

THE Khoja went to get a shave. The barber was clumsy, and each time he plied the razor he cut him and then stuck on a bit of cotton.

When the Khoja reached out his hand to take his turban and go, the barber said, "But you are only half shaved!"

"You clown!" answered he, "on one half of my head you have sown cotton. Leave it alone. Let me sow the rest of it with flax."

The Khoja caught stealing Wheat at the Mill

THE Khoja took some wheat to the mill to be ground. While he was waiting, he proceeded to take handfuls of wheat out of the sacks belonging to the villagers and put them into his own.

"What are you doing there?" demanded the miller.

"Oh! what a fool I am!" answered he. "My wits are all astray."

"If you are such a fool," said the miller, "why don't you take the wheat from your own sack and put it into that of the villagers?"

"I am stupid enough as it is," said he, "but if I did that I should be a downright ass!"

The Khoja as a Musician

THE Khoja was invited to a party, when one of the guests, thinking it would amuse the company, put a mandoline into the Khoja's hand and begged him to give them a tune.

The Khoja caught hold of the instrument and struck the wires from top to bottom, producing a horrible, rasping noise.

"Stop! stop! Khoja!" they cried. "That is not the way to play. To bring out the

THE KHOJA PERFORMS ON THE MANDOLINE.

melody you must move your fingers up and down until you find the proper keys."

"My fingers could not find them at first, but now they have; and I shall be very careful not to move them again! Twang! Twang!"

The Bastinado

NASR-ED-DIN KHOJA was sitting with Tamerlane when they brought in a drunken soldier.

"Give him three hundred blows of the bastinado," cried Tamerlane, and then he saw the Khoja smile.

This made him angry and he called out, "No! Five hundred! Give him five hundred!"

The Khoja burst out laughing, and Tamerlane, starting up like a burning brand from the furnace, shrieked out the words, "Then give him eight hundred!"

At this the Khoja began to rock with laughter, which made Tamerlane dance with rage and cry, "You—who call yourself an authority on the Sacred Law—you clown with a turban like a mill-stone, how dare you mock at me when I give sentence—I, a mighty conqueror who has made the world tremble! What a cold and cruel heart you must have to be still laughing!"

The Khoja replied, "You are quite right in one respect. I do know how serious a matter this is, and I quite agree that you are a bloodthirsty tyrant, but I cannot help feeling surprised at one thing. Either you do not know how to count or you are what your name 'Timour' implies—a man of iron and not a creature of flesh and blood. You know absolutely nothing about the Sacred Law for which you are so zealous. The law allows a maximum of eighty blows for drunkenness *—if so, what becomes of your eight hundred? It is very easy for you to give orders, but you should at least take the trouble to think whether they can be carried out."

---

* *Drunkenness.* If a Moslem drink wine and two witnesses testify to his having done so or his breath smell of wine, he may be beaten with a maximum of eighty blows.

KHOJA GOES HUNTING WITH TAMERLANE

The Khoja goes Hunting with Tamerlane

THE Khoja came on a visit to Tamerlane, who one day gave him a broken-winded hack to ride and took him out hunting.

It came on to rain, so the huntsmen put spurs to their horses and rode for shelter. As the Khoja's horse could scarcely walk, it certainly could not gallop, and he remained behind. He took off his clothes and sat on them. After a while, when the rain left off, he put them on again and in due time arrived at the inn.

When Tamerlane noticed that the Khoja had not got wet, he asked him the reason.

The Khoja said, "Who could get wet riding a spirited animal like that? Directly the rain began, I gave him one touch with the spur and he carried me like a bird straight to the inn."

Tamerlane was so astonished that he at once gave orders that the horse should be put in the Royal stable.

Again they went out hunting. Tamerlane rode the horse and, curiously enough, it came on to rain again. The Khoja and the others put spurs to their horses and soon reached the inn, but Tamerlane was soon wet through and arrived quite late.

Next day he sent for the Khoja to give him a dressing-down.

"How dare you," said he, "tell me a lie and make a fool of me?"

"My dear man," said the Khoja, "there is no reason to be so angry. Have you not your wits about you? You would not have got wet if you had taken your clothes off as I did, kept them dry by sitting on them, and then put them on again when the rain left off."

The Khoja appointed "Judge's Shadow"

WHEN the Khoja was at Konia he applied to the Judge for an appointment as Cadi * in one of the provincial towns. The Judge told him that there was no vacancy, as all the appointments had just been made.

He then applied for employment at head-

---

* *Cadi.* See p. 42. The term is properly only applied to the judge of a small provincial town. At the principal town of a province the judge is called "hakem."

THE KHOJA APPOINTED "JUDGE'S SHADOW"

quarters, but the Judge always found some excuse for refusing.

At last the Khoja said, "Since your Honour has always treated me with kindness and did in fact promise to give me the first suitable appointment, allow me to point out that there is a post vacant. No one has applied for it, no one is keen about it, and certainly neither the Government nor the people can have any objection to it. You will find it very useful in your work, for it will save you many difficult questions which you cannot settle yourself."

"Very good!" said the Judge. "Let me know at once what it is, and I will make the appointment."

"I want you to appoint me to be your shadow," said the Khoja.

The Judge and his staff were intensely tickled at the idea of such a title, and the Judge said, "Certainly! I hereby appoint you to be my 'shadow,'" and showed him a room which he could use as an office.

The Khoja took the matter quite seriously, went into the room, and having placed a desk with writing materials in one corner, took his place, and from that day entered upon the regular discharge of his duties.

One man had a claim against another and brought him before the Judge, who asked what it was about; whereupon the plaintiff said, "This man cut thirty loads of wood for Siraj-ed-din Effendi, who is, as your Honour knows, very rich, and as he was cutting it I passed by, and each time that he drove in the axe I cried 'Hengh! hengh!' to encourage him and give strength to his arm. I gave him very material help. He has just been paid for his work, but refuses to give me anything for helping him."

The Judge turned to the defendant and asked if the plaintiff had indeed done so, and he acknowledged that he had. The Judge was greatly puzzled to know how to treat the matter and felt quite nonplussed. While thinking it over he suddenly remembered his "shadow," and turning to the plaintiff, said, "This is not a question for my department. The gentleman in the room opposite attends to questions of this kind," and he told the Marshal of the Court to take them there. The Judge then hid himself behind the curtain which led into the Khoja's room,

THE KHOJA APPOINTED "JUDGE'S SHADOW"

being very curious to hear how he would deal with the matter.

After hearing the facts of the case the Khoja said to the plaintiff, "Of course you are right. The idea of his receiving all the money, while you stood by and took so much trouble every time he drove in the axe! It is not to be thought of!"

The defendant cried, "But, sir, it was I who cut the wood. What possible claim can he have because he stood there looking on?"

"Hush, my man!" said the Khoja—"you don't understand," and he told his servant to bring him a money-tray. He then took from the man who had cut the wood the money which he had received for the work and proceeded to ring out the coins one by one. He then turned to the man who had cut the wood and said, "Take your money"—"and as for you," said he, turning to the other, "take the sound of the coins as I rung them on that tray, for that is all you will get."

Those who were present during the hearing of the case were very much astonished at this odd way of settling it.

TALES OF NASR-ED-DIN KHOJA

Selling Pickles

ONCE the Khoja started to sell pickles. He bought the entire stock-in-trade of a man, including his donkey. He started on his rounds, crying, " Pickles for sale ! " but when they came to the crowded part of the town and to the house of a former customer, the donkey would begin to bray so loudly that the Khoja could not make himself heard, and was obliged to hold his tongue.

One day in a crowded thoroughfare the Khoja was just preparing to cry, " Pickles ! " when the donkey got the start of him and began to bray. Then he lost his temper and said, " Look here, mate, are you selling them, or am I ? "

A Suit for Payment of " Nothing "

TWO men came before the Judge and pleaded as follows :—

Plaintiff : " Your Honour, this man had a load of wood on his back, and as he was walking along, his foot slipped. He fell, and all the wood came down with him. He

A SUIT FOR PAYMENT OF "NOTHING"

begged me to put it on his back again, and I asked him what he would pay me for doing it? He answered, 'Nothing.' I said, 'All right. I agree to do it for nothing,' and I put the wood on his back. I then asked him for payment of 'nothing,' and he will not give it me. Your Honour, I demand my rights. Let him pay me 'nothing' here and now!"

The Judge always handed over delicate questions like this to our friend the Khoja, who, having listened attentively said, "Your claim is just. He must keep his word. He shall pay."

Then pointing to the rug on the divan, he said to the claimant, "Just lift that rug a bit and tell me what is under it."

The man looked, and answered, "Nothing."

"Why," said he, "that is what you want. Take it and go!"

The Khoja's Conviction that he was Dead

THE Khoja was one day outside the town when he was seized with the conviction that he was dead.

He laid himself out and waited for a long time, but no one took the trouble to remove his body.

He was very much annoyed, and at last got up and went home to tell his wife how and where he had died, and having done so went back to the fatal spot.

His wife ran off to the neighbours, tearing her hair and crying bitterly as she told them that the Khoja had died suddenly and his body was lying out in the open country.

The neighbours were very much distressed and asked when and where it had happened and who had brought the news.

"The strange thing is," she answered, "that it was the Khoja himself who brought me word, and he then went back to the place where he died!"

Dispute in Court between Two Low Women

WHEN he was Cadi of Sivri-hissar two impudent women came into Court. One said, "Your Honour, I asked this woman to make me some cord and paid her in advance. She began to make it very thin—

DISPUTE IN COURT

just like string—and sent me a sample, but I won't take it if it is like that. So do please make her give me back my money." As she said this she began to make soft eyes at the Khoja and to show off her charms.

"Dear me!" he said, as he turned to the other, "and what have you to say?"

The woman affected to speak as if she could not control her indignation.

"Our agreement, sir, was that I should make cord the thickness of my finger, like a clothes-line—not rope, the thickness of my wrist." And so saying she bared her arm to let him see what a pretty white hand she had.

"Oh, that is enough!" said he, as he scanned them both from head to foot. "Settle the matter between you."

To the defendant he said, "You must make it a little thicker. Don't make it so thin that you will find next morning that it has worn out, like my patience."

At this the hussies began to laugh and left the Court.

TALES OF NASR-ED-DIN KHOJA

The Khoja conducts his Own Funeral

ONE day the Khoja climbed up a tree and began to cut the branch upon which he was standing.

A man below saw what he was doing and called out, "Hullo there! Whatever are you up to? You are going to fall."

The Khoja paid no heed, and at that very moment the branch snapped and he came down with a crash. He jumped up, however, immediately, without waiting to see if he were hurt, and rushed after the man.

"Upon my word, young fellow, you are very clever," said he, catching hold of him. "Since you could tell that I was going to fall, please say when I shall die."

The man shook him off and, wishing to proceed on his way, gave the Khoja this cryptic answer: "Put the wood on the donkey's back and as he goes uphill he will throw up his heels and let fly at you. That will half kill you; but when he does it a second time, it will be all over with you." And so saying, he passed on.

The first time the donkey let fly at him the Khoja thought he felt the symptoms of

THE KHOJA CONDUCTS HIS OWN FUNERAL

approaching dissolution, but at the second time the poor man collapsed. "Alas! I am a dead man," he cried, and gave himself up for lost as he fell to the ground.

People from some villages hard by came upon the Khoja lying there prostrate and apparently lifeless.

"The poor fellow is dead," said they, gathering round him. Then they brought a coffin and put him in.

Now, as they were carrying him to town they came upon a steep, muddy swamp. Here the road divided, and although they could see several ways across, they could not make up their mind which was best. They talked the matter over, saying, "I wonder which is best, this or that?"

As they did so, the Khoja popped his head out of the coffin, and said, "When I was alive I used to go that way," pointing with his hand; "but you do just as you like."

The Scalding Soup

ONE day the Khoja's wife, being in a bad temper, put the soup on the table scalding hot.

After a while she forgot that it was so hot and swallowed a spoonful. The pain made her eyes fill with tears.

The Khoja asked her why she was crying without apparent reason, and she said, " My poor mother was very fond of this soup. I remembered it, and that made me cry."

The Khoja at once took a spoonful with great respect and swallowed it, and his eyes also filled with tears.

" What is wrong ? " said his wife. " Why are you too crying ? "

" I am crying," said he, " that your unlucky mother should have died and a wretch like you be still alive ! "

The Khoja's Parable for Young Children

THE Khoja had a charming way of treating little children. At Akshehir they would come round him, delighted to listen to his pretty stories, or they would laugh and play with him. If they had any little trouble they would run with it to the Khoja.

So it came to pass that one day they bought some walnuts, and as they could not agree

THE KHOJA'S PARABLE FOR YOUNG CHILDREN

how to divide them, they came to the Khoja and begged him to do it for them.

The Khoja said, "Do you wish me to divide them as God would do it, or as man?"

The children all answered in the innocence of their hearts, "As God would do it."

The Khoja then took two handfuls and began to distribute them. To some he gave many, to some he gave only one, and to others he gave nothing at all.

Of course they could not understand this and asked him why he did it.

"My young friends," said he, "the reason is quite plain. Supposing that I were to divide you all up into groups as I have done with the walnuts. Look at that boy over there. His father, Bedi-ud-din Effendi, is a very rich man, one of the notables of Akshehir, has a good wife and several fine children. Now look at Sinan-ed-din, that poor little mite who stands next to him. His father is very poor, and they are not happy at home. The man himself is a cripple and will never be able to do much work, and his wife is ill. Look again at Hasham-ed-din standing opposite to him. His family is in different circumstances from either of these. In fact, not one of you is the same as the other and your Khoja least of all.

"There are no bounds to the goodness of God. He has given his servants a mind to think; He has shown them what is good and what is evil, what is wholesome and what is harmful. He has showered them with every grace to enable them to make a right use of their brains, their senses and bodily powers. He who does not know how to make a right use of them will get nothing. Hence the difference in the way God distributes His gifts."

An Impious Petition

THE Khoja had to receive some money from a man who lived a long way off. Being hard up, he went to him and demanded payment, but the man answered that he had not a copper coin in the house.

The Khoja came away disgusted, and as he trudged along the road became very hungry. Suddenly he came upon a baker's shop, where he saw beautiful brown loaves fresh from the oven.

His hunger made him forget himself. He

AN IMPIOUS PETITION

caught hold of a loaf on the edge of the counter and carried it off to a willow tree down the road. He sat there in the shade and looked up to Heaven. "O Lord," he said, "Thou knowest that I am hungry and have not a penny in my pocket, and that I have money to receive from Ahmed Ago. Thou art Omniscient, Almighty! Please pay the baker two piastres for the bread on account of what Ahmed owes me."

Having said this prayer, he proceeded to devour the bread.

A Dissertation on Physical Phenomena

A FOREIGN professor came to Akshehir and approached Tamerlane with a request that he might be permitted to hold a public enquiry as to certain questions which he wished to propound. "If," said he, speaking through an interpreter, "you have learned doctors, discreet and skilful in debate, let us have a meeting for the purpose."

Tamerlane called the notables together and said, "A foreign professor has come to your country and he wishes to hold a public enquiry into questions connected with physical science. These men are great travellers. If you cannot bring to meet him a professor who is gifted with a knowledge of science, wherever he goes he will spread it abroad that the learned classes in Anatolia are of no account, and that will injure your good name among the nations."

Thereupon the notables held a consultation, at which after long reflection they came to the conclusion that there really was no such professor in the country; but they said, "This will never do. We must think of something. We must avoid such a calamity!"

They had a long talk and discussed the possibility of bringing a professor from Konia or Kaiserieh.

At last one of them remarked, "It will take a long time to get a man from outside the district—let alone one who speaks foreign languages. I am afraid this is going to bring us into disgrace with Tamerlane and make us unpopular."

"Come now," said another, "let us hear the opinion of our learned Khoja on the subject. Maybe we shall manage to confound

A DISSERTATION ON PHYSICAL PHENOMENA

this clown of a foreigner by some queer trick of his."

Finding this an excellent idea, they sent for the Khoja and explained the matter. He at once said, "You leave it to me. If I can shut him up by an apt reply, it will be fine; but if I cannot, all you have to say is, 'Oh! that fellow! He is cracked—a half-witted Khoja who came to the meeting unbidden. Don't take any notice of him.' Then you will have to find some other educated person to meet him. If I succeed, I shall look for a good present from each of you, and of course I shall get a reward from Tamerlane."

"O Khoja," said they, "God give you whatever you ask so long as you can save our faces in the eyes of this stranger!"

The end of it all was that on an appointed day tents were pitched in the public square and the ceremony was made august and awe-inspiring by the presence of Tamerlane and his Court, all covered with gold and jewels and armed with the full panoply of war. Next came the foreign professor, a mop-headed, queer-looking fellow, who was given a seat near his Majesty.

After the people had settled down into

their places, everyone sat waiting for the arrival of the Khoja. At last he entered, wearing an enormous turban and a gown with open sleeves. He brought with him his pupil Hamad with two other students and he was given a place on the left of his Majesty.

After drinking sherbet and a moment's repose, the professor stepped forward and drew a circle on the ground. He then looked into the Khoja's face for an answer.

The Khoja at once rose and with his stick drew a line right through the centre of the circle, thus dividing it into two parts. He then looked at the professor and, seeing that he approved, proceeded to draw a line across in the opposite direction, thus dividing the circle into four parts. With a wave of the hand he made a gesture as if he would draw three of the parts towards himself, while he pushed the other towards the professor. Then he looked again at the professor, who expressed his approval and congratulations by waving his hand.

After this the professor held his hand in the form of an open tulip. Holding his fingers outstretched he waved them several

A DISSERTATION ON PHYSICAL PHENOMENA

times in the air (fingers up). The Khoja also made a gesture exactly the reverse so that his fingers pointed to the ground, and the professor made a sign of approval.

Then the professor pointed to himself and with his fingers imitated an animal walking on the ground. Then he pointed to his belly and made a gesture as if he were pulling something out.

The Khoja now took an egg from his pocket and, shaking his arms, imitated the act of flying. The professor approved this also, and, standing up, he made a profound obeisance to the Khoja, kissing his hands. He then told the interpreter to congratulate Tamerlane and the notables on possessing such a treasure as Nasr-ed-din Khoja.

The spectators were delighted. Each one in turn congratulated the Khoja on having saved the honour of the country and showered on his head the presents which they had provided for the occasion.

Tamerlane also enriched the Khoja with generous gifts.

After everyone had left, Tamerlane, attended by his retinue, took the professor on one side and said to him through the inter-

TALES OF NASR-ED-DIN KHOJA

preter, " We could not understand anything from your dumb-show. What was it you said ? What kind of answer did the Khoja give you which made you retire from the contest ? "

The professor explained his object in the following words :

" Greek and Jewish professors are not agreed on the subject of the Creation, and as I did not know the opinion of the learned Doctors of Islam on the subject, I was very anxious to ascertain what it was.

" Consequently I first showed that the world was round. The Khoja not only accepted this fact, but by those lines which he drew he first marked the Equator, dividing the globe into a northern and southern hemisphere. He then drew a line across the centre of the circle at right angles to the first, and by taking three of the divisions to himself and leaving one to me he meant to say that three parts of the globe are water and one part dry land.

" Then, in order to show the different species of animals and probe the secrets of Creation, I waved my fingers up in the air, intimating thereby the production from the

A DISSERTATION ON PHYSICAL PHENOMENA

earth of vegetables, trees, springs, and minerals. The Khoja replied by pointing his fingers downwards, showing clearly, and in agreement with the most recent investigations, that these things are produced by the rain from Heaven, affected also by the sun's rays and the influence of other celestial bodies.

"Then I pointed to myself and indicated by a gesture that all creatures on the face of the earth are propagated one from another. I had, however, left untouched quite a large proportion of living things.

"The Khoja now took an egg from his pocket, held it out and then made a movement as though he were flying, alluding beyond all doubt to the bird species. He hereby gave a full and comprehensive answer regarding the Creation of the world and the propagation of species.

"From this I saw that your Khoja is a most talented professor who embraces in his personality a knowledge of science both celestial and terrestrial. Therefore the people of Akshehir in particular and his fellow-countrymen in general may well be proud of such a sage."

After taking leave of the foreign professor with due respect and honour, they collected round the Khoja and asked him to explain the matter—and this was his answer:

"Pooh! Call him a professor indeed! The fellow was a poor, sick, dog-hungry starveling. You need not have worried about him! When I came he drew a circle as you saw him do. 'Oh!' said he to himself, 'if only it were a tray full of cakes!'

"I first divided the circle into two parts, meaning that I would share the cakes with him. But I saw that he did not understand, so I divided it into four parts, taking three for myself and giving him one.

"The poor fellow was satisfied and waved his hand as if he would say, 'Oh! we would be all right if a pot of pilaff* were boiled and put on the tray!' and I made a gesture as if to say, 'Yes, and we would flavour it with pepper and salt, pistachios and raisins.'

"Then he pointed to his stomach, by which he meant to say, 'Ah! if you only knew what a long distance I have come and how long I have wished for a good meal!'

---

* *Pilaff*. A dish of boiled rice (or crushed wheat) flavoured with chicken broth or meat gravy.

"I, in dumb-show, answered, 'But I am more hungry than you. I am so light on an empty stomach that I could fly like a bird. I got up this morning and my wife gave me only one egg for breakfast. You sent for me and I had not even time to eat it. I put it into my pocket as a stop-gap.' There you have the whole story."

Setting a Light to the Furze on the Donkey's Back

HE put a load of furze on his donkey's back, and then said to himself, "I wonder whether furze, when it is damp, can be made to blaze and burn just the same as when it is dry." So saying, he set light to it on one side, and as there was a pretty stiff wind blowing at the time, it caught at once on all sides.

It made a terrible crackling noise and a great shaft of flame shot up into the sky.

Of course the poor beast went wild with fright and bolted along the road, braying and kicking up its heels.

When the Khoja saw that he could never catch it up, or even get near it, he shouted out at the top of his voice, "To the lake, you fool! If you have any sense in your head, run to the lake!"

Climbing a Moonbeam

ONE night while in bed, the Khoja heard a thief walking on the roof. He said to his wife, "Last night I came home and knocked at the door, but I couldn't make you hear, so I said this prayer . . ., and catching hold of a moonbeam I got into the house."

The burglar, who was listening to the conversation through the chimney, repeated the prayer to himself, then caught hold of a moonbeam with both hands and let himself go. He had hoped to get down quietly, but he fell from the roof with a crash and broke his bones.

The Khoja ran at once and collared the burglar, calling out to his wife:

"Quick! Quick! Bring a candle, I have caught him."

The burglar, being unable to move, said quietly, "Please don't be in such a hurry! What with your prayer and my own stupidity here I lie unable to escape."

AN ASS'S COLT BORN WITHOUT A TAIL

The Khoja as a Letter-writer

A MAN came to the Khoja and said, "Do me a favour. I want you to write a letter for me to a friend at Bagdad."

"Oh! don't bother me," said he. "I have no time now to go to Bagdad."

He was walking off when the man ran after and stopped him. He was curious to know what he meant.

"My dear Khoja," said he, "why should your writing this letter for me make it necessary for you to go to Bagdad?"

The Khoja answered, "There is nothing strange about it. My handwriting is very bad. I am the only person who can read it, so that if I write a letter for you I must be there to read and explain it!"

An Ass's Colt born without a Tail

AS the Khoja was leaving home he said to his wife, "My dear! cook a nice pilaff of bulghur* for supper and we will have a jolly evening together.

* *Bulghur.* See footnote on page 29.

He came home tired, threw off his cloak, and feeling very hungry rushed to the table, where he noticed that his wife had laid out a dish of youghourt* and spring onions in addition to the pilaff.

"Bravo! little wife!" he cried, and sitting down began to eat with great appetite and good-humour.

They were full of laughter and merriment when the child of the people next door came running in, looking very unhappy.

"Oh, please come, sir," he said, "mother wants you. We are in great trouble and there is no one can help us but you!"

The Khoja, who had a tender heart, at once jumped up and ran next door.

Half an hour afterwards he came back looking very much annoyed, and when his wife asked what it was he said, "Just think of it! You and I were enjoying a pilaff such as I have not seen these forty years, and am called away because the ass next door has given birth to a colt without a tail!"

* *Youghouri.* Milk coagulated, but not curdled rather acid but very wholesome and refreshing. The best "youghourt" is made from sheep or buffalo's milk

SOCIAL AMENITIES

Social Amenities—An Act of Discourtesy

ONE of the notables of Akshehir was notorious for the great respect with which he treated Nasr-ed-din Khoja, and he had so often begged him to pay him a visit that one day the Khoja felt he must do so.

When he came to the house and looked up he saw the great man at the window, but directly he caught sight of the Khoja he turned his head away and disappeared.

The Khoja knocked at the door and said to the servant, "I hope it is not inconvenient, but I have come to see your master."

"Oh, what a pity!" was the answer. "Master has just gone out, and he will be so sorry when he hears that you came."

The Khoja was naturally very much annoyed and called out loud, "Very good; but just tell your master not to leave his head on the window-sill the next time he goes out. It is not of the slightest consequence, but when a man is taken in by your master's fine compliments and repeated requests that he should pay him a visit, and, in order to do so, has to leave his business, and after all is treated with such discourtesy, he curses him and will have nothing more to do with him."

A Strange Way of Riding a Donkey

ONE day, as the Khoja was riding to the Mosque to give a lesson he sat on his donkey with his face to the tail, his pupils walking behind.

They asked him why he made himself so uncomfortable, riding in that fashion.

"You see," said he, "that if I rode with my face looking straight ahead, you would be behind me. If, on the other hand, you were to walk in front you would turn your backs upon me. I think, therefore, it is better to ride this way. It is more polite!"

Tamerlane in Hell

A GROUP of people sat talking, and their conversation turned upon the next world and the terrors of the Judgment-day.

While they sat there brooding over the matter, Tamerlane, who was sitting next to

TAMERLANE IN HELL

the Khoja, heaved a deep sigh and said to him, "O Khoja, what will become of me on the Judgment-day? Shall I have a seat in Heaven or Hell?"

"Really, your Majesty, I am sorry to see you vex your Royal heart with such matters. In my humble opinion, you should not worry nor have the slightest doubt on the subject. When Jenghiz Khan and Hulagu died, it is quite clear that they must have gone straight to Hell. Oh, yes! your Majesty may be quite sure that you will have a seat of honour there along with Nimroud, Pharaoh, Alexander, and Jenghiz Khan."

The Khoja cannot read Persian script.

A PERSIAN from Azerbijan received a letter in Persian, and happening to meet the Khoja asked him to read and explain it.

The Khoja took it in his hand and when he saw that it was in Persian and written in broken script (Shikasté), said, "You must get someone else to read it," and handed it back.

As the man persisted, the Khoja said, "I am not very familiar with Persian, and even if this were written in Turkish, I could never make it out."

The Persian waxed indignant and said, "You are a pretty fellow! You don't know Persian and you don't even know how to read! What right then have you to call yourself a Khoja and go swaggering about with a turban on your head like a mill-stone?"

At this the Khoja lost his temper, tore his turban from his head and his cloak from his back and threw them to the Persian, saying, "There you are. Put them on. If that is all that is necessary in order to read the letter, let me see you read a line or two yourself."

The Khoja and the Jew

AT one time while saying his morning prayers the Khoja would call out:

"Lord! Lord! Give me a thousand pounds; but if it turns out to be one pound short, I won't take it."

His next-door neighbour was a Jew. This man constantly heard the Khoja saying this, and it made him very curious, so he put 999 pounds into a bag and threw it down

THE KHOJA AND THE JEW

the chimney while the Khoja was repeating his prayer. He then began to listen, saying, "I wonder what he will do?"

The Khoja first returned thanks to God that his prayer had been heard, then took the bag with the greatest reverence, counted the money, and found that there were only 999 pounds. He calmly put the bag into his pocket, saying, "God, who has given me the 999 pounds, will certainly make up the difference."

When the Jew saw this unexpected turn of events, he got into a terrible state of mind and ran to the Khoja's house as soon as it was daylight, saying to him, "Enough of your joking, Khoja. Give me back that money of mine."

The Khoja answered quite seriously, "Money? What money, Jew? Have I ever asked you for money? Did you ever put money into my hand?"

"But it was I," cried the Jew, "who threw that money down the chimney! Every morning I heard you repeat the same prayer, and I said to myself, 'Let me see whether the Khoja will keep his word.'"

The Khoja laughed sardonically and said:

"A fine cock-and-bull story! Do you believe it yourself—that a Jew would, for an experiment, throw such a large sum of money down my chimney? No!" said he calmly, "God has given it to me in answer to my prayers."

The Jew, seeing that the matter would never be settled between them, said, "Very well, let us go to the Court."

"I have no objection at all," said the Khoja, "but I cannot go on foot."

So the Jew brought him a fine mule.

"Then," said the Khoja, "I have appearances to keep up. How can I appear before the Judge in this old cloak?"

So to avoid delay the Jew brought a valuable fur pelisse and put it on the Khoja. Then he mounted him on the mule and so they went to the Court-house.

When the Cadi asked what they wanted, the Jew said, "Your Honour, this man owes me 999 pounds and refuses to pay."

The Cadi turned to the Khoja.

"And you, what have you to say?"

The Khoja said, "Ask him, please, if he has ever given me a piastre."

The Jew then told his story, at which

THE KHOJA AND THE JEW

the Khoja laughed, saying, " Your Honour, this man is my neighbour. He probably heard me counting my money. The Lord has indeed given me much, and He is able to give me a thousand times more. As for this Jew, he would rather die than give a piastre to a Mohammedan. He wants to swindle me out of my money. I should not be at all surprised that if you were to ask him he would say that the mule I was riding outside belongs to him."

The Jew, in a fright lest he should lose his mule also, at once called out, " Of course it is mine! It was because you would not come to the Court on foot that I got it for you."

The Cadi began to feel doubtful. The Khoja, noticing this, said, " Why! he will tell you next that he owns the fur coat which I am wearing on my back."

At this the Jew lost all control over himself and shouted, " Yes! I do! The coat is mine also!"

At last the Cadi became indignant, and said, " You rascal of a Jew! You not only try to rob the property of a man so universally respected, but dare to treat our Court

with contempt! Enough! Out you go!"
They turned the Jew out of the Court.

The Khoja went home in state, riding the mule and wearing the pelisse. When he arrived, he sent for the Jew next door, who sat there brooding in despair. He gave him back all his property, and having made him happy, proceeded to give him advice never again to meddle with a compact made between a man and his God, nor to treat His servants with disrespect.

The Jew, after receiving so severe a lesson for having tried to make a fool of the Khoja, was quite overcome and swore he would never again play tricks with a Moslem.

Singing in the Turkish Bath

ONE day the Khoja went to the Turkish bath and finding that he was quite alone began to sing a song called, "Kaya bashi" (Up on the rocks).

He began to think that he had rather a fine voice and said to himself, "If I can sing so nicely I ought to let my people hear me."

SINGING IN THE TURKISH BATH

When he had finished his bath he went straight up to the minaret, and as it was midday began to recite the call to prayer, "Allah-u-Akbar." As he did so a man called out from the street, "Shut up, you clown. What do you mean by shouting the call to prayer in that ugly voice?"

The Khoja leaned over the parapet and said to him, "Ah, if some charitable person would only build a Turkish bath up here, you would soon see what a pretty voice I have."

The Sleepless, Hungry Khoja

THE Khoja had been invited out to dinner. He arrived rather late, when dinner was over, and his hosts were under the impression that he had already dined.

Sherbet was brought in, and after a short conversation they wished him good-night and retired.

The servant then came in, and having made up a luxurious bed for him, left the room.

When he was alone the Khoja began to feel desperately hungry. He tried to forget it and go to sleep. Quite impossible! At last he got into such a nervous state that he began to pace up and down the room. He saw that this could not go on long or he would go mad. So he stepped out of the room and rapped at the vestibule door. Immediately his host ran out in great excitement, crying, "What is it? What is the matter?"

"Sir," said the Khoja, "you have given yourself much trouble on my account. That is a most luxurious bed you have given me, but we are simple folk, inured to poverty, and cannot get to sleep on such sumptuous couches. I would be better pleased if you would give me just one griddle-cake. I would put part of it under my head to serve as a pillow and the rest on top of me to serve as a quilt. Then I shall sleep as sound as a top."

Damages for the Loss of a Cow

WHEN the Khoja was Cadi at Akshehir a man came into Court and said, "Your Honour, while the cattle were out grazing a red cow—I rather fancy it belongs to you—

DAMAGES FOR THE LOSS OF A COW

attacked mine, ripped up its belly and killed it. What is to be done about it?"

The Khoja answered, "The owner is not responsible and you cannot sue the cow for blood-money."

"Oh! I made a mistake," said the man. "I should have said that it was my cow which had killed yours."

"Hah!" said the Khoja, "in that case the matter becomes more complicated. Just hand me down from the shelf that book with the black binding. Let us see how the law stands."

The Khoja's Nightcap

THE Khoja stopped the night with a friend and the servants put on his bed an enormous cotton turban instead of a nightcap.

He untied the sash and fastened it tightly round the middle, saying to himself, "I will undo it in the morning and put it back as it was before." So saying, he lay down to sleep.

He was still in bed when his friend the host came into the room and said jokingly,

"Bless the man! How fond of sleep you are! One would say that you had joined the Seven Sleepers of Ephesus."*

Then he caught sight of this strange-looking object on the Khoja's head and it was some time before he could make out what it was.

"Why, Khoja!" said he, "you have strangled your turban!"

"What else could I do?" said he. "If I had not strangled it, it would have strangled me."

Weeping at the Bedside of his Sick Wife

THE Khoja's wife fell ill, and every day when he returned from his work he would sit by her bedside and weep.

A lady who lived close by came in to enquire after her and said to him, "Do not fret so. There is no reason to be alarmed. Please God, she will soon recover."

"My dear lady," answered he, "I am a busy man. To-morrow I may be off to the village or have something else to do. I

* See Appendix.

have nothing on just now, so I am having a good cry. What else can I do? I may not have a chance later on, and you know the poor thing has no one else but me to cry for her."

Garlic and Honey

A GOVERNOR came to Akshehir who was rather eccentric.

"If anyone knows a good dish," said he, "I wish he would write out the recipe and we will make a Cookery Book."

He made the suggestion to one of the principal men of the town, who passed it on to the Khoja.

Next day the Khoja met this man and said, "Do you know I was thinking all night about what you told me. I have invented a rare dish—one that no one has ever heard of—quite delicious!"

When the man asked what it was, he said, "You must make a batter of garlic and honey."

The man, who was a bit of a fool, went off at once, and happening to meet the Governor, said to him, "We have a Khoja in the town, a man of much experience and quite an original character." He then proceeded to give him the Khoja's recipe.

Now, the Governor was by no means as intelligent as he was supposed to be. He answered, "How extraordinary! You don't say so!" and at once hurried home and gave orders to the cook that he was to try it for supper.

Of course it was disgusting.

The Governor was very angry and told the man who had mentioned the Khoja to him, to bring him to Government House.

"So you are the man who invented a dish of garlic and honey?" he asked.

"Your very humble servant," replied the Khoja, "unworthy though I be to have done such a thing."

"Very well," said the Governor, and gave orders that he should be made to eat some on an empty stomach next morning.

As he turned it over in his mouth he made horrible grimaces at the nasty taste, and the Governor said, "What are you making those faces for? Enjoy yourself. Take your fill

GARLIC AND HONEY

of this dish you invented. Perhaps it tastes differently to the man who made it."

"Your Excellency!" said the Khoja, "this invention of mine was only a theory. I had never tasted the thing before. Now I have, and I see that theory and practice are quite different things. I don't like it, either."

The Cat and the Meat

ONE morning the Khoja bought three okes of meat and left it at the house while he went back to his work.

His wife at once called her friends in and gave them a good dinner with it.

In the evening the Khoja came back to supper and his wife gave him nothing but plain boiled pilaff of bulghul. He turned to her and said, "Even if you had no time to make me something with the meat, you might at least have put a few pieces of the fat in this pilaff."

"Indeed," she answered, "I was just going to do it when I was prevented. Your favourite tom-cat came and ate it all up. I just came in time to see him do it."

The Khoja at once ran to fetch the scales, brought out the cat which was under the charcoal brazier, and weighed it.

It came to exactly three okes!

He turned to his wife and said, "You wretch! If what I have just weighed is the meat, then where is the cat? But if it is the cat, where is the meat?"

The Unpaid Grocer's Bill

THE Khoja owed fifty-three piastres to his grocer and for a long time had paid nothing on account.

One day he sat talking with friends in the market when the grocer passed by and made a sign with his hand that if he did not pay the money he would show him up to his friends.

The Khoja understood what he meant and turned his head away. The man passed again and made the same gesture. The exasperated Khoja shook his head once or twice, muttering "God save me from the rascal!" but the grocer, who was one of those devils who are not to be driven away

THE UNPAID GROCER'S BILL

by prayers, persisted all the more. The Khoja was still muttering, "God help me!" when his friends noticed what was going on. Then, seeing that the man would not go away, the Khoja lost his temper and called to him, "Come now, how much do I owe? Fifty-three piastres? Very good, come to-morrow and I will give you twenty-eight. Come the next day and take twenty more. How much does that make?"

"Forty-eight."

"How much remains?"

"Five."

"You bare-faced rascal! Are you not ashamed to insult me before my friends for only five piastres? Begone!"

Bread and Salt

THE Khoja went to a town and one of the inhabitants said to him, "I have taken quite a fancy to you. Please come and take bread and salt with me and let us have a pleasant chat together."

The Khoja accepted the invitation with pleasure.

After a while bread and salt were put on the table, but nothing else, and the Khoja, being very hungry, had to eat it. Just then a beggar came to the door and begged for something to eat. The owner of the house, who was evidently a terrible miser, put his head out of the window and shouted to the man to go away, adding, "If I have to come to you, I will give you a good thrashing."

When the Khoja saw that the beggar kept on crying out, he, too, put out his head and said to him, "My good fellow, don't you imagine that he is like other people. You cannot humbug him. He is a man of his word!"

Three Thousand Piastres for a Pair of Tongs

ONE day the Khoja was strolling through the market when he saw a broker offering a sword for sale at three thousand piastres. He examined it, but could find nothing remarkable about it, so he turned to some people who were sitting there and asked them why it was so expensive. "Because," said

A PAIR OF TONGS

they, "when used against the foe, it becomes five yards long."

Next day the Khoja took the tongs from the fireplace and went with them to the market.

"Tongs! Tongs! Who'll buy?" he cried. "Going for three thousand piastres!"

Some people heard him and were curious to see what it was. They took up the thing and examined it and saw that it was a common pair of fire-tongs worth about two piastres.

"What on earth is there in this, Khoja, that you should ask three thousand piastres for it?"

He turned to the dealers and said, "Only yesterday you were hawking a sword about the market for three thousand piastres, because, forsooth, it became five yards long when used against the foe. Let me tell you that if my wife were to get angry and hurl these tongs at me, they would become ten yards long, and perhaps more."

Chewing Mastic Gum

THE Khoja had been invited out, and sat with the guests chatting and chewing mastic gum, when a servant came in to say that dinner was ready.

As the guests rose to go into the dining-room the Khoja took the mastic out of his mouth and stuck it on the tip of his nose.

When they asked him why he did it, he answered, "Poor people should always keep an eye on their property."

The Khoja and Muleteers in the Cemetery

ONE day while the Khoja was walking close to the cemetery his foot slipped and he fell into an old grave. He pulled off his clothes, which were covered with dust, and began to clean himself.

Suddenly an idea came into his head. "Let me put myself in the dead man's place and see whether the angels Munkar and Nakir * will come to me."

* *Munkar and Nakir.* Two angels who are said by Mohammed to visit the dead in their graves and examine them as to their belief in Islam. They are described as black angels with blue eyes.

THE KHOJA IN THE CEMETERY.

KHOJA AND MULETEERS IN THE CEMETERY

While he was thinking it over some muleteers drove their animals at a gallop up to the cemetery. The Khoja, who could not make out what it meant—this noise of bells, rushing of animals, and cries of muleteers—said to himself, " What an unfortunate time for me to have come here! It must be the end of the world!"

In his agitation he knew not what to do, but at last managed to scramble to the top of the grave and was on the point of running away when the mules came round the corner and caught sight of him as he sprang out of the grave—a most extraordinary-looking object. They shied and there was a regular mix-up, one falling on top of the other. Their loads—pots, glasses, cups, and plates—were all smashed to atoms.

The muleteers in a towering passion attacked the Khoja with their sticks.

"Who are you? What are you doing here?" said they.

"I?" he stammered—"I am from the other world. I had just come out to see how things were going on."

The Khoja kicked Downstairs

ONE day the Khoja was coming out of doors when his next-door neighbour met him and said, " Oh, Khoja, I have been so uneasy! This morning I heard some excited voices talking and whispering in your house, and then a loud bang. What was it?"

The Khoja showed that he was annoyed, and answered, " I had a little tiff with my wife. She became very angry, gave my coat a kick and it rolled downstairs. That was all."

" But," said his neighbour, " could a coat make all that noise?"

When he repeated the question the Khoja said, "That's enough! Why are you bothering me like this? As a matter of fact, I was inside the coat!"

The Khoja scandalizes the Wedding Party

THE Khoja came home at midday to perform his ablutions before going to the Mosque. He tried to get away in time for prayers, but his wife kept him so busy and he made himself so dirty that she told him he had better go off to the bath for a wash.

KHOJA SCANDALIZES THE WEDDING PARTY

As he left the house she called after him, " Mind you are not late. Remember it is my sister's wedding-day and you have to give her away. If you are not there, you will keep everybody waiting and the guests will be very much offended."

The Khoja found it very tiresome having to take a bath at such a time and made short work of it, but just as he was getting ready to dress and to run back home, they told him that it was raining heavily outside. He looked out and saw that the sky was overcast and that it was not likely that the rain would leave off in a hurry.

So he made a bundle of his clothes, tucked them under his arm, and started off home as naked as a savage; and of course he was drenched.

The wedding guests were all standing before the front door waiting for him, but when they saw him arrive in this state, they exclaimed, " Khoja! whatever do you mean by this ? "

He answered, " The man who has to humour his wife by taking a bath at this time of day, gets both a hot bath and a cold one at the same time."

TALES OF NASR-ED-DIN KHOJA

A Dish of Youghourt for Two

THE Khoja and a friend of his bought some youghourt to be eaten "share and share alike."

They were just beginning to eat it when his friend made a mark across the middle, saying, "I am going to put sugar and salt on my half."

"But this is liquid," cried the Khoja, "and part of it is sure to come over to my side. It won't be nice. If you do put it on, sprinkle it all over, and we shall know what we are eating."

"I have very little sugar," said the other, "and I am not obliged to give you any."

The Khoja got angry and, reaching out his hand to his knapsack, took out a bottle of salad oil and at once began to pour it on.

"What!" said the man. "Salad oil! Who ever heard of putting salad oil into youghourt!"

"What is it to do with you? I am going to pour it on my own half. I shall do as I please, and as for you, look after your own part."

"But," said the man, "is it possible to

A DISH OF "YOUGHOURT" FOR TWO

put anything into a liquid which will not go from one side to the other?"

"Don't play the fool then!" said the Khoja. "Put the sugar in the middle!"

The Khoja is caught stealing in a Garden

ONE day the Khoja went into a garden and took all the melons, carrots, and turnips he could lay his hands on. He was busy filling his bag with them when the gardener suddenly appeared.

The Khoja was very frightened, and when the gardener asked what he wanted there, he answered in his confusion, "That fearful storm we had last evening caught me and threw me in here."

"Indeed!" said the gardener; "and who picked these things?"

"Well, you see," said the Khoja, "as the wind threw me this way and that, everything that I caught hold of stuck to my hands."

"A very pretty story indeed," said the gardener again; "but who has been filling the bag?"

"H'm!" said the Khoja, "that is just what I was wondering!"

He pulls the Moon out of the Well

ONE moonlight night the Khoja went to draw water from the well and saw that the moon was inside. He at once fastened a hook on to the rope to pull it out. As the rope dangled, the hook caught on to a stone. The Khoja began pulling with all his might, but as the hook got clear he fell on his back.

Then he saw the moon was up in the sky.

"Ah! thank God!" said he. "I had a tough job to do it, but the moon is back in its place."

The Quails

THE Khoja shot a large number of quails, which he dressed and put on to stew. He clapped the lid on the saucepan and went out to invite his friends to dinner, wishing

THE QUAILS

to give some of them who were always questioning his skill an agreeable proof of it.

While he was out, another man came and carried off the cooked quails, putting live quails in their place.

The Khoja's friends arrived, the saucepan was brought out, and the Khoja proudly took the cover off; the quails flew out with a flutter and disappeared. The Khoja stared in amazement, and then ejaculated:

"Oh Lord! granted that Thou hast restored the quails to life and made the dear little creatures happy again, how about my butter, salt, pepper, herbs, cooking expenses, and all my hard work? Who is going to pay for them?"

The Importunate Creditor

WHILE looking out of the window the Khoja saw a man crossing the street to whom he owed some money—a debt of very long standing.

"My love!" said he to his wife, "run downstairs and when he comes, stand in the doorway and tell him what I told you to say

TALES OF NASR-ED-DIN KHOJA

the other day, and I hope he won't come and bother me again for a long time."

His wife went down, but he felt curious and followed her to the door to hear the conversation.

The man knocked, and the Khoja's wife, peeping through the doorway, asked what he wanted.

"Madam, by this time you must know by my voice who I am. I have called a hundred times about this money which the Khoja owes me. It is scandalous. Tell him to come here and I will give him a piece of my mind," said he angrily.

The Khoja's wife answered gently, "My husband is not at home, but you can give me any message for him you wish. You are quite right, sir, to complain; but we are so sorry that we have not been able to get the money yet. However, little by little, we shall try to scrape it together. My husband intends to plant a hedge in front, and as the sheep from the village are always passing our door they will rub themselves up against the hedge and so we shall get a lot of wool. We will clean it, card it, spin it into yarn, and then sell it to pay your money.

THE IMPORTUNATE CREDITOR

"We are not the sort of people to do others out of their money. Oh dear, no!"

The man saw very plainly that he would never get his money back, but was so tickled at this odd way of making it that he burst out laughing.

Tamerlane and the Accounts

TAMERLANE, having ascertained that the Governor of Akshehir was very rich, determined to confiscate his property on the pretence that he had defrauded the public revenue, and summoned him to appear before him.

When he presented his accounts, which were written on cardboard, Tamerlane tore them up and made him swallow them. He sequestered his property and stripped him of everything, to the very last farthing. Then he sent for the Khoja and issued an order appointing him Controller of Inland Revenue on account of his reputation for strict integrity.

The Khoja pretended that he was not very well, but Tamerlane wouldn't listen to any excuse.

At the beginning of the month he called upon him for a statement of his accounts; but when he saw that the Khoja had written them out on a griddle-cake he began to laugh, and said, "Why, Khoja, what is this?"

"Oh!" answered he, "wouldn't you make me swallow them sooner or later, as you did the other fellow? I have not got such a fine appetite as he had. I am an old man and can only digest this. No cardboard for me!"

The Nobleman and the Khoja's Wife

ONE day the Khoja's wife and some other women went to the shore of the lake to do some washing. It chanced that the lord of the district attended by his servants was walking in the same direction. He began to stare at the women, seeing that they were unveiled and lightly clad, when the Khoja's wife called out, "You impudent fellow! What are you staring at?"

At this the nobleman turned to his servants and asked whose wife she was, and they told him.

THE NOBLEMAN AND THE KHOJA'S WIFE

Next day he sent for the Khoja.

"Is that your wife," he asked—"the woman dressed in blue, tall and ruddy?"

"Yes," said the Khoja.

"Then send her to me," said the nobleman.

When the Khoja asked him what he wanted her for, he answered, "I want to ask her something."

"Well, ask *me*," said the Khoja, "and I will go and ask *her!*"

The Ordeal

TAMERLANE was in search of an Ottoman Turk of approved courage to fill high office at Court. One might of course find a brave man, but it needed special courage to serve on his staff. It would be at the risk of one's life and no one ventured to apply for the post. And yet it was quite impossible to tell Tamerlane that there was nobody, so they applied to the poor Khoja, who was always ready to make himself a scape-goat.

"Oh! please, Khoja," they said. "You

are the only man in the town he cares for. You know how to get round him. You know his little ways. If only for a short time, do please accept, and later on we will see what is to be done."

After every possible argument they at last persuaded the soft-hearted but patriotic Khoja. He gave them his promise, and they informed Tamerlane. The latter knew right well that the Khoja had plenty of courage, but as he required the services of a man who had also physical strength he gave his consent provided that the Khoja should first undergo a certain ordeal. He gave orders accordingly, and they made the Khoja stand erect in an open space in the presence of Tamerlane, who directed one of his archers to fire an arrow so as to pass between the Khoja's legs. Though very much frightened, the Khoja did not utter a sound, but began to mutter all the prayers for the dying he could think of.

Tamerlane then told the Khoja, who wore a cloak with wide sleeves, to stretch out his arms at full length and ordered another archer to shoot an arrow so as to pierce the cloak under the left arm. The poor Khoja

THE ORDEAL

was in an agony of fear; and by the time Tamerlane ordered a third archer to shoot an arrow through the knot which fastened his turban, he felt quite faint and dazed. However, thanks to the wonderful skill of the archer, he came off unscathed.

Then they congratulated him on having passed his examination, and he revived. He would not let them see how tired he was, and even began to smile.

Tamerlane was loud in his approval of the Khoja's courage and endurance, and not only showed his appreciation by the presents which he gave him, but having been informed that there were holes in his cloak and turban, gave orders for him to be supplied with new ones.

The Khoja expressed his thanks for this favour and then said, "May it also please your Majesty to give orders that I may have a fresh supply of underlinen, so that I may have a complete new outfit."

"But, Khoja," replied Tamerlane, "I am informed that no damage was done by my men to your underclothing. They examined it and did not notice anything."

"Your Majesty is quite right," said the

Khoja; "but although there are no outward signs, I greatly fear that they have been damaged inside."

Selling his Turban at Auction

ONE morning the Khoja was trying to fasten his turban, but could not get the end to fall behind as it should.

He undid it and tried again, but it was no use. At last he lost patience and sent it to be sold by auction.

One unhappy wretch made a bid for it.

The Khoja went up to him and whispered, "Mind what you are about. Don't bid too high, or it will be knocked down to you. It is quite impossible to get the end to fall behind!"

Gives Thanks for the Loss of His Donkey

THE donkey was lost. The Khoja ran about trying to find it and at the same time giving thanks in a loud voice.

He was asked why he gave thanks, and he

COUNTING THE DAYS OF RAMAZAN

answered, "Because I am not riding it. Of course, if I were, I would be lost too."

Counting the Days of Ramazan

WHEN the fast of Ramazan began, the Khoja said to himself, "Why should I keep my fast the same as others do? I will get a big jar, and each day I will put one stone into it. When there are thirty stones in it I will keep the feast of Bairam."*

He found a jar and started to throw one stone in every day. His little daughter saw him do this and she threw in a handful. One day some people said to him, "Khoja, what is the day of the month?"

"Wait a bit! I will go and see and let you know," said he.

He went home, emptied the jar, began to count, and saw that there were exactly one hundred and twenty stones. He said to himself, "If I go and tell them exactly what these stones tell me, they will think I

---

* *Feast of Bairam.* The feast which follows the fast of Ramazan. The people put on gay apparel, visit, embrace and kiss each other, exchange presents, feast and keep holiday for three days.

am a fool!" So he made up his mind, went back to them and said, "It is exactly the forty-fifth day of the month"; but they answered, "Why, Khoja, a month can only have thirty days!"

"Well," said the Khoja, "I was very moderate in what I said to you. If you were to see the account which I keep in that jar, you would find that to-day is the one hundred and twentieth day of the month.

The Loan of a Cauldron

ONE day the Khoja asked a neighbour for the loan of a cauldron. After he had done with it, he put a small saucepan inside and took it back to the owner. When the man saw the small saucepan, he said, "What is this?" and the Khoja answered, "Your cauldron has had a baby."

"That's good news!" said the man, and accepted it with pleasure.

One day the Khoja wanted to borrow the cauldron again and took it home with him.

The owner waited a long time, but he noticed that the cauldron did not come back.

THE LOAN OF A CAULDRON

Then he went round to the Khoja and knocked at his door. When the Khoja came and asked him what he wanted, he answered, "I want that cauldron."

"Accept my sincere condolences," said the Khoja, "the cauldron is dead!"

"What!" said his neighbour in the greatest amazement—"dead? Whoever heard of a cauldron dying?"

"Strange!—strange!" replied the Khoja. "You could believe that the cauldron had a baby, and yet you do not believe that it could die!"

Tamerlane disguised as a Dervish

AT the time of the conquest of Anatolia by Tamerlane the Mongols occupied the district of Akshehir, and as a result of their brutal tyranny the towns were empty and the villages and open country thronged with panic-stricken women and children. The Khoja too mounted his wife on the donkey and, taking his boy along with him, went to a secluded village in the hills.

One day five or ten refugees and people

from the village were gathered together near the fountain holding an excited discussion about the tyranny of the Mongols and their brutal character. The Khoja joined in and began to detail the awful torments which these tyrants would have to suffer in Hell from the wrath of God, when a Dervish who had been quietly looking on burst out suddenly with a voice of thunder, " No, Khoja ! You may know everything about the Koran and Sacred Traditions, but not about those who are the Sword of Divine Vengeance and patterns of Divine Justice ! God loves not such people as you in whom the strain of patriotism has become corrupt —poor-blooded folk, listless, lazy, disunited, woman-hearted ! "

This Dervish was a man of forbidding aspect, tall, dark-complexioned, hook-nosed, with a long face and scanty beard and black eyes with a keen, searching glance. He wore a high black cap with a long tassel which covered his eyebrows, and a cloak, while in his hand he carried a beggar's wallet. The people, startled by his terrible voice, were seized with panic. Some of them threw themselves to the ground, while others

TAMERLANE DISGUISED AS A DERVISH

remained staring, aghast at the motionless figure of the Dervish.

The Khoja gave him one searching look from head to foot and began to feel quite faint. "I wonder," said he to himself, "can it possibly be he?"

Then with a courage born of despair he asked, "From what country are you? Would you kindly tell me your honoured name?"

In the same terrible voice the Dervish replied, "I am a pilgrim from Tartary. My name is Timour."

When he said *that* the Khoja quite lost his head. "And do you put the word Khan after your name?"

As the terrible being answered, "I do!" the Khoja turned to the people and cried, "Away! ye people of Mohammed. Begone to your prayers—the prayers for the dead!"

Geese at Akshehir have only One Leg

ONE day the Khoja cooked a goose and took it as a present to Tamerlane. On the road he could not restrain his appetite and ate one of the legs. On arrival at the palace he presented his offering in due form, but Tamerlane noticed that there was one leg short and asked him where it was. The Khoja replied, as cool as a cucumber, that all the geese at Akshehir had only one leg. " If you don't believe me, look at those geese standing over there by the fountain ! "

It was quite true. The geese were all standing on one leg, sound asleep in the sunshine, the other leg tucked up and their heads sunk in their breasts.

Tamerlane looked out of the window and saw that they really had only one leg.

Now, it chanced to be the moment for changing the palace guard. The band struck up. The roll of the big drum and skirl of pipes made the welkin ring. The geese soon found their second legs and ran off helter-skelter, trying to escape. Tamerlane saw them and at once called the Khoja to the window saying, " You are a liar. You see they all have two feet."

" Yes," replied the Khoja, " and if you had the noise of those drum-sticks ringing in your ears you would grow four legs."

A Wager: The Khoja's Vigil

ONE night in mid-winter when there was a very hard frost the Khoja's neighbours made up their minds that, by hook or by crook, they would make him give them a dinner.

"Come now, Khoja," they said, "we want to have a bet with you. If you win, we will stand you a first-rate dinner; but if you lose, you are to give us a pilaff, helwa* and anything else you like."

"What is it?" asked the Khoja. "Is it anything I can really do?"

"No! Of course not!" said one of them. "What would be the use of having a bet if you could?"

The Khoja began to feel nettled and said, "Come now, what is this wonderful thing which I cannot do?"

The man said, "You have to stand up all night in the public square, and in the morning we will all meet at the big Mosque. If you can do it, the dinner is yours. But remember! you will have to stand upright in the open air in a frost which is sharp

* *Helwa.* A light paste of flour, butter, and sugar.

enough to split marble, and as to fire, the mere idea of it is out of the question. So think it well over before you decide, for however brave a man may be, it is not everyone who can stand it. Remember that you cannot get under shelter for a while and then come back to the place, because the houses of Hassan and Mehemet Effendi look upon the Square and their women-folk will be watching you until morning."

The more the man talked the angrier the Khoja became.

"I don't care a rap if a whole regiment of soldiers keep watch," said he, "I am a man of my word and I'll do it. So that is enough!"

Then one of them said with a mocking smile, "What a brave hero! So you really think you can? On one side of the place where you have to stand is the Cemetery. Just think of that! Don't come afterwards and say we persuaded you! Say good-bye to your wife and children. If anyone owes you any money, or if you have any money put away anywhere, tell *me*. If you owe any money, ask Ahmed Effendi to see to it. His back is broad enough to bear it."

A WAGER: THE KHOJA'S VIGIL

"I should be a silly ass to do anything of the kind," said the Khoja. "I don't care a rap. I have quite made up my mind. I'll let you see that the Khoja has a frame of steel and a heart of marble. I am accustomed to roughing it. Many is the time I have slept in as hard a frost out on the road or up the mountain pass. Thank God! there is nothing to fear—no wolves and no brigands. As for the silent dead, I am on better terms with them than anyone. I daresay I have slept in a graveyard quite a thousand times. As for saying good-bye and making my will, that is all nonsense. I am not leaving anyone behind to inherit my goods or anything undone, to be done to-morrow; and as for money, you all know that I do not care about it. With me it goes like water."

Seeing that they could not dissuade him, they chose the place in the Square where he was to stand, and left him.

In the morning the Khoja met them at the Mosque as fit as a fiddle and full of fun. They asked him how he had passed the time, and he told the story in the following words:

"Everything was white with snow. There

was not a sound save the howling of the tempest, not a movement save the swaying of the trees and the crash they made as they fell one upon the other. About a mile off, somewhere—I could not quite make out where—the light of a candle could be seen."

When he said this one of them called out, "That won't do! We agreed that there was to be nothing like fire up there, but you were warming yourself all the time by the light of that candle. You have not kept the agreement!"

The others at once backed him up and decided that as the Khoja had broken the agreement he must give the dinner.

In vain he protested that their claim was absurd. They stifled his voice and would not hear a word, so that he saw it was useless to resist.

On the appointed night all the guests arrived, evening prayers were said, and they sat down to beguile the time with conversation. Two o'clock struck, but there was no sign of dinner.

They became impatient and said to the Khoja, "Never mind waiting until it is quite cooked. Bring it in as it is."

A WAGER: THE KHOJA'S VIGIL

"I cannot possibly do that," said the Khoja. "Have a little patience."

They made two or three more attempts to persuade him, but when three o'clock came the guests began to press him so rudely that he said, "All right!" and left the room, as they thought to bring it in. They waited a while longer, but as he did not come back they said, "The rascal is having a game with us. Let us see what he is up to."

They went into the kitchen to look for him, but there was not a sign of the Khoja or anything to eat. Then they went out into the yard and saw that the Khoja had hung an enormous cauldron to a tree and put a candle under it while he sat looking on with a grin on his face.

"Whatever do you mean?" they cried. "This is beyond a joke!"

"Well," said the Khoja, "you see I am cooking your dinner!"

"Good heavens!" they answered, "you hang a cauldron up in the open air and light a candle under it! Do you possibly imagine that a pot could boil with only a candle or even a torch under it—and at such a distance?"

"Really!" said he, "how soon you have forgotten! Only three days ago did you not all decide that I had been warming myself by the light of a candle a mile off? Compared with that I should say this gives out more heat than a Turkish bath. If it be possible to warm oneself by the light of a candle one mile away, cannot a candle give out enough heat to warm a cauldron only a few feet away?"

It is said that after the Khoja had paid them out by playing them this trick he gave them dinner and they spent a merry evening together.

A Safe Hiding-place for Money

NASR-ED-DIN KHOJA had a sum of money, and one day when there was no one in the house he dug a hole and buried it. He had gone as far as the door when he looked back at the place and said, "If I were a burglar I should find it at once," so he removed it and buried it in another spot. Then he stepped back and examined this also, found that it was not suitable, and hid

A SAFE HIDING-PLACE FOR MONEY

the money in another place. And yet he was not easy in his mind.

Just in front of the house there was a mound. The Khoja went into his garden, cut a stake, tied the bag of money to the end of it, then went to the top of the mound and drove the stake in. Then he came down and had a look.

At last he felt satisfied. He said to himself, "Man is not a bird that he should be able to fly up there. What a capital place for it!" and so saying, he went away.

A thief had been watching the Khoja, and no sooner had he gone than he climbed up the mound, pulled out the stake, and took the money. Then he spread some cowdung on the top and put it back in its place.

After a while the Khoja wanted some money. He went up to the stake to look for it, and found that the bag had disappeared but that there was some cowdung on the top.

He said to himself in utter amazement, "Well, I never! I said no man could climb up there, but how has a cow managed to get to the top? What a strange affair!" said he, shaking his head.

TALES OF NASR-ED-DIN KHOJA

Tamerlane's Title

TAMERLANE said to him, "You know, Khoja, that all the Caliphs of the Abbaside* line had characteristic titles. One was called 'Moaffik-billah,' another 'Motawakkil al-Allah,' another 'Motassem-billah.' If I had been one of them I wonder what would have been mine?"

The Khoja replied at once, "O Lord of the world! there is no doubt about you. Your title would have been 'Naouz-billah'" ("God save us from this man!").

When a Man Marries his Troubles Begin

THE Khoja was having a house built and he ordered the carpenter to put the floors on the ceilings and the ceilings on the floors.

The man asked him why, and he said, "I

---

* *Abbasides.* A dynasty of Caliphs descended from El Abbas, son of Abu-l-Muttalib, paternal uncle of Mohammed. He overthrew the Omayyad Caliph of Damascus, Merwan II, and established the dynasty of Bagdad.

"RAIN COMES FROM GOD"

am going to be married. When a man marries his troubles begin. Everything is soon upside down. Far better do it now than have double expense later on."

"Rain comes from God"

ONE rainy day the Khoja was sitting indoors, and as he looked down the street he saw one of his neighbours pass by in a great hurry for fear of getting wet, and asked him why he was running. He said he was trying to escape from the rain as he did not wish to get wet.

"Oh fie! For shame!" said he. "Rain comes from God! The idea of running away from it! I am ashamed and sorry to hear this. Whatever is the world coming to!"

The poor man went on his way, but evidently felt ashamed of himself, for he began to walk slowly. The Khoja watched him go with a cynical smile on his face, for of course the man reached home wet through.

By a strange coincidence the same man was looking out of his window one rainy day and saw the Khoja run past, although only one or two drops had fallen. He had tucked up his skirts and was running like greased lightning.

"Hullo, Khoja," he cried, "have you forgotten the little reminder you gave me the other day? The idea of running away from God's rain!"

The Khoja paused for a moment and said, "I am running because I don't want to tread God's rain under foot," and he rushed into his house, slamming the door behind him.

One Pomegranate for Each Question Answered

A MOLLAH met a literary gentleman and asked him to explain certain questions. He told him that the only person who could do so was Nasr-ed-din Khoja of Akshehir.

It happened that the Mollah had to pass by Akshehir on his journey, and that outside the town he came upon a man dressed in a turban, wearing sandals and driving a plough. It turned out to be the Khoja himself. He went up to him, salaamed, and said he had some difficult questions which he wished to ask him, and was proceeding to do so when the Khoja saw that he had some very fine pomegranates in a handkerchief.

"Stop!" said he, "I will answer your questions if you give me those pomegranates."

For each answer he took one pomegranate until there were none left.

"There is just one more question," said the Mollah.

"Not if I know it!" said the Khoja; "you have no pomegranates left," and so saying he went back to his plough.

The Khoja and Hamed go Wolf-hunting

ONE day he went to hunt the wolf and took with him his pupil Hamed.

The latter was very keen on getting a young wolf and made his way into the den.

The wolf happened to be outside and was just rushing in when the Khoja caught hold of his tail and held tight.

The wolf began to struggle, and Hamed, who did not know what was going on outside, but felt the dust going into his eyes, cried out, "What are you making so much dust for, Khoja?"

He answered, "If once the wolf gets his tail free, you will see not only dust—you will see Hell!"

Inshallah! *(Please God)*

ONE night the Khoja was chatting with his wife and said, "To-morrow, if the weather is wet I mean to go out cutting wood, but if fine I shall go ploughing."

"Say Inshallah! (please God) when you talk like that," said she.

"Not at all," said he; "I shall certainly do one or the other."

As he was leaving the town next morning he met a troop of soldiers. One of them called to him, "Gaffer, come here. Show us the road to Carabash."

The Khoja answered roughly, "I don't know it."

"Hah!" they cried, "you impudent fellow!" and before the Khoja could find time to speak they began to beat him. "We'll show you what's what! Now step out and show us the way!" and they drove him along as he ran barefoot in front of them. It rained and he was quite wet when he brought them to the village.

He got back home at midnight, sick, footsore, almost half dead.

When he began to knock at the door his wife called out, "Who is there?"

He answered, "Oh! little wife, it is I, Inshallah" (Please God).

Tamerlane's Dream

TAMERLANE dreamt that he had killed a man who treated him with disrespect.

No sooner did the Khoja hear of it than he packed up his traps and fled to the village. The people said to him, "Khoja, you are the only man who can manage him. Whatever you do or say he never gets angry. We cannot do without you. Why did you leave him and come away?"

The Khoja answered, "By God's grace I am able to cope with any situation when he is awake. If I cannot get what I want, I at least act as a check upon him; but when he is dreaming I dare not interfere. I should get more than I bargained for."

TALES OF NASR-ED-DIN KHOJA

Conscience-money

WHEN the Khoja was a student a rich man gave him five hundred piastres with a request that he would pray for him at the end of each " Namaz."*

The Khoja immediately took out fifty piastres and handed them back saying, " Sir, the nights are short and I sit up gossiping so late that (God forgive me!) I cannot get up in time for morning prayers, so I take an extra snooze instead. Consequently I am ashamed to take pay for them."

Who shall feed the Donkey?

THE Khoja grew tired of feeding the donkey and told his wife that in future she must look after it. This she refused to do, and there was such constant wrangling over the matter that at last they agreed to hold their tongues, and that the first one who spoke should feed it.

The Khoja retired to a corner of the room and for hours together kept an obstinate

* See Appendix.

WHO SHALL FEED THE DONKEY?

silence. His wife was so annoyed that she put on her veil and went next door.

Towards sunset she was sitting there telling her neighbour all about it. "He is such an obstinate fellow," she said, "that he will die of hunger. What do you say? How would it be if we sent him some soup?"

They decided to do so, and calling a boy sent him round to the Khoja with a basinful.

It happened that when the Khoja's wife left him to go next door a burglar broke into the house and proceeded to make a clean sweep of everything. He went into the room where the Khoja was sitting and saw that he took not the slightest notice of the noise he was making. At first he felt rather scared, but when he saw that the Khoja paid no attention, making no answer when he spoke to him, but sat there like a graven image, he said to himself, "He must have had a stroke of paralysis!" and without more ado, proceeded to gather up everything useful that he could lay hands on.

The burglar was so tickled at the behaviour of the Khoja that he said to himself, "Let me pull his turban off his head and see if that won't make him speak!" He did so, but the Khoja did not stir, so he put the things on his back and went off.

Just after he left, the boy came, and seeing the image sitting in the corner, said, "They have sent you some soup, sir."

The Khoja at once tried in dumb-show to make the boy understand that the house had been robbed, that even his turban had been carried off, and that his wife ought to come back at once. He made a hissing noise with his mouth, and, pointing to his head, passed his hand round it three times.

The boy understood by this that he was to turn the basin three times round and then clap it on to the Khoja's head. He did so, and of course the poor man was drenched. The soup and bits of meat made a horrible mess all over his face, going into his eyes, hair, and beard.

The Khoja, however, would not speak nor stir.

The boy went back, and in answer to questions told them what he had seen—that the doors, cupboards, and boxes were all open, and things all lying about in confusion—and he also told them what he had done with the soup.

The Khoja's wife realised that something very serious had happened and at once ran home.

When she saw the damage which had been done she rushed up to the image who sat there grinning in the corner and cried out passionately, "What is the meaning of all this, Khoja?"

"Ha! ha!" said he, "go off and feed the donkey. It was your obstinacy which was the cause of all this."

Question of Precedence at Public Prayers

THE Khoja visited a Koordish tribe to perform the office of Imam during the fast of Ramazan.

When conducting public prayer his place was of course in the very front of all; but one day the sons of the Koordish Bey came to him and said:

"Khoja, of course we have no wish to hurt your feelings by making you hold your tongue, but you really go too far. Not once, but five times or more you have dared to take precedence of our father, the Bey. One would say you think we are nobody, but our father has five thousand men-at-arms ready to do his will at a moment's notice, and you presume to take precedence of such a mighty man as that! Be careful! Don't think that because he has not yet said anything about it, he never will. The time may come when he will get angry, and who then can save you from his clutches?"

They gave it him hot and strong.

Now, although the Khoja still tried to impress upon them the necessity for public prayer, he got such repeated warnings from the young princes that at last he said to himself, "I must see what is to be done."

The matter worried him so much that he decided to speak to the Bey on the subject and so put a stop to the interference of his sons.

In the evening he broke the fast with the Bey, and after they had taken a glass of mastic together the Khoja thought it a good opportunity to speak.

"Sir," said he, "the young princes—no doubt with the object of guarding your honour, but also because they are ignorant of

PRECEDENCE AT PUBLIC PRAYERS

the obligations of the Sacred Law——" and then stopped short, for the Bey frowned and said:

"What is it, Khoja? Is it about the meeting for public prayer?"

The wretched Khoja now repented a thousand times over that he had ever raised the question. He shrank into himself and said, "Yes, sir; but I did not wish to make a complaint—God forbid! I only mentioned it by way of conversation."

"Khoja," said the Bey, "they had no business to have spoken to you about it, but —mind you, I say this because I like you— you take great liberties with me."

When the Khoja, who had counted on the Bey's protection with the greatest confidence, found that he was treated in this high-handed fashion, he made up his mind that as soon as the fast was over he would take his fees and clear out as soon as possible. He answered however, "You are quite right, sir; but I venture to submit that one should never think of where a man stands first, but where he stands last. Shall I not, when the fast is over, stand before you as a suppliant? Will you not stand before me, the poor Khoja, as the mighty Koordish Bey, while I shall stand alone at the back of the crowd?"

The Bey paused awhile in thought; then his brow cleared, and he said to the Khoja with a smile, "Ah! Khoja, you see that we are a people who live far from the haunts of civilization. How can we grasp such subtle logic as this?"

Tamerlane and the Figs

TAMERLANE, after defeating Sultan Bayazid at the great battle of Angora, spent some time at Akshehir, where he was on very friendly terms with Nasr-ed-din Khoja. It was due to the Khoja's influence that the people of Akshehir were saved from massacre, and he often intervened to prevent harsh measures being taken against them. This, however, is by the way. I want to speak of some of the little jokes that passed between them.

I remember especially that one day the Khoja put three plums on a tray and was taking them as a present to Tamerlane when, as he went along the road, the plums kept falling off.

TAMERLANE AND THE FIGS

The Khoja kept on saying, "Behave yourselves. Stop playing, or I will eat you! However they would not listen, but went on rolling and toppling over. At last the Khoja got in a rage and ate two of them. The other he presented to Tamerlane, who was very pleased and gave him a good present in return.

A few days after the Khoja put some beetroot into a basket and was taking them to Tamerlane when he met a man on the road who asked what he had in the basket.

"A present for the Ameer," said he—"a basket of beetroot."

"I think," said the man, "he will be better pleased if you give him some figs."

So the Khoja got some fine figs and presented them to the Ameer, who ordered his servants to pelt him with them.

As the figs broke on his head and stuck to his face the Khoja kept muttering, "Thank the Lord! I shall know in future how wise it is to take the advice of another man."

When Tamerlane heard him he asked what he was giving thanks for.

"Well, your Majesty," said he, "I was bringing you some beetroot, but I met a man on the road who recommended me to bring these figs. I thank God because if I had brought the beetroot I really cannot think what would have become of me. I should have had my head broken, my eyes knocked out, and have been smashed to bits!"

The Heart of a Tyrant

A CERTAIN Tyrant, while stopping at Akshehir, went for an inspection to a village where his soldiers were quartered and stayed away one week. When he came back the Khoja called upon him and said, "Well, how did you get on? Did you enjoy yourself?"

"Oh, yes," he answered, "I had a most enjoyable time. It happened that on the Monday a fire broke out in the village. I saw it all. There were some lives lost. Fancy! One man lost his mother-in-law, and he really seemed to be sorry.

"On Tuesday a mad dog bit two men. They burnt them with hot irons to prevent their going mad also. They bellowed like buffaloes.

THE FLOOD.

THE HEART OF A TYRANT

"On Wednesday there was a flood. A lot of houses fell. The water was covered with furniture and odd things—among them a cradle with a child in it, floating on the water like a boat. The flood carried off cows, calves, and camels. That kept me busy until the evening.

"On Thursday a bull broke loose. He wounded five or six people, knocked out the eye of one man and ripped open the belly of another. They told me that he was not expected to live.

"On Friday a villager in a fit of frenzy murdered his own children. That made me very angry. I had the rascal put to death by torture. That kept me busy till quite late.

"On Saturday a very large old house suddenly fell with a crash. Men, women, and children lay buried under the ruins. One could hear their screams all over the village. I had the rubbish cleared away a bit; but as the house was only built of earth, the bits of furniture quite useless, and the wounded were quite horrible to look at, I thought it better not to save them, and so they perished. Most of them died uttering piercing cries.

"On Sunday a woman hanged herself on a plum tree. We went to see that too. She left one little girl in the cradle.

"In short, every day of the week we had something to amuse us."

The poor Khoja, utterly unnerved at hearing these stories, and feeling quite faint, said with a voice quivering with indignation, "Thank God you came back soon! If you had stayed there another week, thanks to you, not one stone would have remained upon another."

"*To-morrow may be the Judgment Day*"

THE Khoja had a pretty little lamb which he would never let go out of his sight and he fed it with the greatest care. Its gambols were a constant source of amusement to him. Some of his friends had cast their eyes upon the lamb and made up their mind that by hook or by crook they would get it from the Khoja and eat it.

One of them came and said, "Khoja, the end of the world is coming. It may be to-day or to-morrow. If so, what will you do

"TO-MORROW MAY BE THE JUDGMENT DAY"

with that lamb? Bring it along and let us eat it."

The Khoja took no notice, and then another friend came and tried the same game, but the Khoja sent him about his business. However, they kept on bothering him until he got sick of it, and agreed to give them a picnic in the country on the following day. The lamb was killed and the fire lighted and the Khoja began to turn the spit. His friends took off their cloaks and vests and handed them to the Khoja to take care of them while they went off in different directions to play games.

The Khoja, who had the painful duty of roasting his pet lamb, seized the opportunity and threw all their clothes into the fire. After a while they came back from their sports, hungry for dinner, but what did they see?—all their clothes burnt to ashes!

When they rushed up to the Khoja, yelling out, "Who did this?" he answered, "Why! my lads, what a fuss you are making! To-morrow may be the end of the world. What will you do with clothes then?"

TALES OF NASR-ED-DIN KHOJA

The Khoja's Horse is "Left-footed"

THE Khoja was once travelling with the caravan. Early in the morning everyone began to get on their horses in a hurry.

The servants brought the Khoja's animal up to the horse-block, and he, putting his right foot into the stirrup, swung himself up and of course landed on the horse with his face to the tail.

"Oh, you clumsy man!" they cried, "you got up the wrong way!"

"Not at all!" answered he. "It was the horse. It is left-footed!"

The Khoja tossed by an Ox

THE Khoja had an ox—a big, powerful brute with a pair of horns that moved like springs. Whenever he came back from harvesting, he would feel a longing desire to take a ride on those horns.

"Oh!" said he, "if only I might sit there and grasp them with my two hands, and away!"

This became a fixed idea with him.

THE KHOJA TOSSED BY AN OX

One day he saw the ox asleep in the yard and quietly sat down on its forehead, saying to himself, "What a capital opportunity!"

The ox showed a nasty temper, lifted the Khoja and tossed him to the ground. He rolled over on his head and lay senseless.

His wife came up, and seeing him lying there, thought he was dead and began to cry. After a while he opened his eyes, and seeing that his wife was crying, said, "Don't cry, little wife. Of course I have had rather a bad time of it; but after all, I got what I wanted."

An Embarrassing Question

THE Khoja had two wives. One day they came in together and began to tease him, saying, "Which of us do you love best?"

The unhappy man felt very much embarrassed, and though he said "I love you both" and tried to show that he was impartial, they were not content, but continued to press for an answer.

At last the younger of the two said, "Now, suppose that both of us were in a boat on the Akshehir lake and that as we were approaching the shore it capsized and we both fell in. Suppose you were standing on the shore, which of us two would you save first?"

The Khoja was as startled as if the thing had really happened and, quite involuntarily, turned to his old wife, saying, "I think you know how to swim a little bit, don't you?"

He mourns for his Donkey—not for his Wife

THE Khoja's wife died, but he showed not the slightest sign of grief. Some time afterwards his donkey died, and his friends noticed that he was terribly distressed.

Some of them asked him the reason, saying, "You did not mourn like this when your wife died; but it is ten days since you lost the donkey, and you are still going about with a clouded brow."

"Ah, yes!" said he. "When my wife died, the neighbours came to condole with me, saying, 'Don't fret, Khoja! We will find you another, far better than she was'; but when the donkey died, no one came to give me comfort like that. Have I not good reason to grieve?"

The Khoja slaps the Judge in Court

A MAN hit the Khoja a blow on the back, and when he turned round sharp to see who it was, the man said, " I beg your pardon, I thought you were one of my pals."

The Khoja collared hold of him, dragged him into Court, and made a complaint before the Cadi.

It appeared, however, that the man was the Cadi's friend. He received a summons to attend on a certain day, and when he came into Court the Cadi turned to the Khoja and said, " Give him a slap too, and so you will be quits."

But as the Khoja was dissatisfied, the Cadi said, " Then the man must pay a fine of one piastre. Off you go," said he. " Bring the money here, and we will pay it to the Khoja as compensation."

The man went off, and the Khoja waited for hours, until he was convinced that the Cadi had allowed him to escape.

He watched for an opportunity, and when he saw that the Cadi was deep in thought, gave him a slap, saying, " Your Honour, I cannot wait any longer. Take that, and collect the fine of one piastre from the man," and off he went.

Measuring the Earth

ONE day some people met him and said, "Come, Khoja, you know a thing or two. We are very much puzzled to know the size of the earth—how many feet or yards it measures."

Just then a funeral passed by, and the Khoja pointed to the coffin, saying, "The man who can answer your question lies there. Ask him, for he has just taken its measure."

A Way to make the Donkey Go

THE Khoja passed by the place where the fishermen were caulking their boats. He asked them why they had lighted a fire and what they were doing to the boats.

"Well, you see," said they, "we burn the bottom of the boat a little bit and then we rub in the tar. That makes the boat sail fast."

A WAY TO MAKE THE DONKEY GO

"Ho! ho!" said the Khoja to himself, and directly he got home he took out the donkey, put hobbles on its feet, and fastened some brushwood on to its tail. No sooner had he set light to it than the donkey broke his hobbles and bolted.

"Ha! ha!" cried the Khoja. "There's a donkey for you! Before I had time to rub in the tar, off he goes!"

The Khoja and the Fox

ONCE while the Khoja was a student he made a tour of the villages in search of employment as Imam during the Fast. At every village he met with a polite refusal. "How do you do?" they said. "So glad to see you, but sorry we have already engaged our Imam."

After calling at five or six villages he came to one which had been much harassed by the depredations of a fox. There was not a chicken or turkey left in the place, and it had even carried off the villagers' boots and shoes—in short, the damage was inconceivable.

At last they laid a trap and, after no end of trouble, caught it.

When the Khoja arrived, the villagers were holding a meeting to discuss the particular tortures by which they would put the fox to death.

As he came up to them they said, "Oh, what damage that cursed brute has done! But, thank Goodness, we have caught it and we are now talking of taking our revenge by putting it to exquisite torture."

"No! no!" said the Khoja; "you leave that to me."

"Well, well," they said to each other, "he must be a man of some experience—far more so than we are."

So they stepped aside and began to watch the Khoja, who at once proceeded to take off his cloak and undo his belt, with which he tied the cloak fast round the fox's belly. Then taking his turban, he tied it tight on the fox's head and let it go.

"Whatever have you done?" cried the villagers as they made a dash to try to catch the fox again.

But the Khoja stopped them, saying, "You listen to me! I have inflicted upon him a torture more horrible than any of you can conceive. Whatever village he goes to dressed like that, they will say, 'We have nothing for you,' and drive him away."

The Khoja is carried off to the Mortuary

THE Khoja left home early one morning for one of the villages, where he had some business to look after.

It happened that a public entertainment had been arranged for that evening, and as the Khoja's presence was indispensable, because he was such good company, some young fellows made a plan to prevent him going.

The Khoja got all ready for the journey and started off to join the caravan, but on the way he was held up by these people, who demanded where he was going.

"I am off to the village of Heritan for a few days on business," said he.

"Poor wretch!" they answered. "It is your last journey in this world. You are a dead man, and it is our duty to see that you are properly buried. Some of us look up to you as our Khoja, some of us are your relatives, others are old cronies of yours, but all of us are your friends."

So saying they caught hold of him and dragged him off to the Mosque.

The Khoja, who was always frightened out of his wits at the very thought of death, began to struggle and cry,

"Oh, let me be! Drop this stupid joke. If you carry it any further it will become sober earnest and I shall indeed die. I really have important business at the village, so let me go on and join the others. You know that if I don't catch them up I cannot go alone."

However, they paid no heed to his entreaties and stifled his cries. At last he lost all power of speech. They bundled him into a coffin and were just going to close the lid when they caught sight of one of their friends going off in another direction. They at once called to him. "Hullo! there. The Khoja is dead. You must come with us to the funeral."

The man said he was busy, but they insisted.

While they were wrangling about it the Khoja raised his head and said to the man,

KHOJA IS CARRIED OFF TO THE MORTUARY

" It is absurd for you to struggle. My business was much more urgent than yours, but what is to be done? I am dead. The people are all waiting for me in the Mosque, and you—well, you must go too. You cannot help yourself."

He dreams that he is being forced to marry again

THE Khoja dreamt that the ladies of the parish came and were standing round him trying to persuade him to marry a woman, and saying, " She is just the one to suit you ! "

He woke up blushing and gave his wife a dig in the ribs to wake her. " Get up, you lazy thing ! " said he. " Fancy lying there and taking no notice. Don't you see that the ladies of the parish are all here trying to marry me by force ? You will be getting a partner. Go and drive them away. If you don't, you'll only have yourself to blame. Don't say then I didn't warn you ! Remember that the old wife always has to take a back seat ! "

TALES OF NASR-ED-DIN KHOJA

Mistaken Identity—A Confusion of Thought

ONE day a man came up to the Khoja and stood gossiping for a long time. As he was going off the Khoja said, "Excuse me. I do not think I know you. Who are you?"

"Then why," asked the man, "have you been talking to me all this time as if I were an old acquaintance?"

"I noticed," answered the Khoja, "that both your cap and your cloak were like mine, so I thought that you must be myself."

The Khoja as a Lad Perverse and Intractable

WHEN the Khoja was a lad he always did exactly the opposite of what his father told him to do. His father therefore found that his best plan was to tell him to do just what he did not wish him to do.

They were returning from the mill one day and had to cross a stream. There was a bridge, but it was out of repair and unsafe for animals to pass.

"I am going across by the bridge, my lad," cried his father, "but mind, you are not to take the donkey across the ford."

KHOJA AS A LAD PERVERSE, INTRACTABLE

Of course young Nasr-ed-Din at once began to drive the donkey across, but his father could see from the bridge that the sack of flour was all on one side, so he shouted out, "The sack is not hanging over on my side. It is not going to fall into the water. Don't put it straight, whatever you do. Shove it a little bit more this way!"

Young Nasr-ed-Din shouted, "Father, I have always done exactly the opposite of what you told me to do, but this time I am going to do what you say." He had scarcely touched the sack before it rolled off into the water.

The Lost Saddle-bag

THE Khoja stopped at a village where he lost his saddle-bag. He at once sent word to the villagers, saying, "If you do not find it and bring it back, I know what I will do."

As the Khoja was a man of some reputation and not to be trifled with, the villagers were very much alarmed. They had a good search and found it.

One of them, however, was curious to

know what the Khoja would have done if they had not found it.

"If you had not found it?" he answered coolly. "Oh! I have an old rug at home. I would have pulled it to pieces and made another."

Carrying the Blind Men across the River

ONE day the Khoja was sitting on the river-bank when ten blind men came along. They made a bargain with the Khoja that he should carry them over for one para* apiece.

He took them on his back one at a time, but when half-way across he let one of them fall and the flood carried him off.

Then the blind men began to cry out; but the Khoja said, "Noisy fellows! What are you making all this fuss about! I have had quite enough of you. Pay me one para short and have done with it."

* *Para.* About a quarter of a farthing.

THE FEAST OF TANTALUS

The Date-stones

THE Khoja was eating dates, and his wife noticed that he did not take out the stones.

"It seems to me that you are not taking out the stones," said she.

"Of course not," said he. "When I bought them the greengrocer did not allow for the stones when he weighed the dates. Had he thrown them away, he could not have sold his dates; and as I paid cash down, do you think I am going to throw them into the street? Not I! Whoever told you I was so wasteful? I paid for them, have eaten them and found them very good, so that is enough!"

The Feast of Tantalus

ONE of the notables invited the Khoja to Iftar.* He went to ask him quite early in the day, then took him round from

* *Iftar* is the breaking of the month's fast on the eve of the Bairam. It is also applied to the breaking of the fast every evening.

one mosque to another until he became desperately hungry.

As they entered the dining-room he saw stuffed turkey, baklawa, and cakes on the sideboard and felt that he could hold out no longer. As they took their places his mouth began to water.

First some excellent tripe soup was served, and the host with great ceremony proceeded to taste it.

"Drat the man!" he cried. "Kiaya!* come here at once! How often have I bid you tell the cook not to put garlic into the soup? Take it away at once!"

The Khoja looked after it wistfully and gently tightened his belt.

Then turning to him his host remarked, "It is quite impossible to make these cooks understand. They will do as they like, whatever you say to them."

A chorus of voices answered, "They will indeed."

At this moment the turkey was put on the table. It was done to a turn and smelt delicious. The stuffing was made of raisins, rice, and pistachios, and there

* *Kiaya.* Head servant, butler, or major-domo.

THE FEAST OF TANTALUS.

THE FEAST OF TANTALUS

was so much of it that it went all over the dish.

The host took a small piece, but he had no sooner done so than he cried out furiously, "Aga, come here! Did I not tell you the other day to see that the rascal does not use spice? Do you do this on purpose? Thirty years you have been in my service and yet you allow this to go on! God pay you out for this! Take it away!"

Out went the turkey, and the poor Khoja heaved a deep sigh as he saw his sheet-anchor disappear.

Then a eunuch brought in the baklawa, but the host scowled at him and said, "You stupid Arab! Do hungry people begin with sweets? Away with it!"

As the whip fell on his shoulders, the poor fellow let the dish fall and bolted from the room.

The Khoja, seeing all these tempting dishes carried out one after the other, took his spoon and catching hold of a dish of pilaff which was on a side-table, began to devour it.

"Hullo! what are you doing there, Khoja?" cried the host.

"Oh! sir," said the Khoja, "do give me a

chance before you condemn it to the same fate as the others. Let me have a little talk with my old friend the Pilaff—ask how he is and find out what he has inside him! Never mind me!"

At this the guests began to roar with laughter. The dishes were then brought in again, they set to work in earnest and made a merry meal.

Spectacles required to see a Dream

ONE night he woke his wife in a great state of excitement. "Quick!" said he—"be quick. Give me my spectacles before I wake up." She handed them to him, but asked why he was so excited.

"I am having a beautiful dream," he answered, "but there are one or two things in it I cannot make out very clearly."

How the Earth may "Turn Turtle"

A MAN asked him, "Why is it that when morning comes some people go off in one direction and others in another?"

"Because," said he, "if they all went in one direction the earth would lose its balance and turn turtle."

A Recipe for cooking Liver

ONE day the Khoja bought some liver, and as he was carrying it away a friend met him and asked how he meant to cook it.

"Oh! as usual," answered he.

"No!" said his friend, "there is a very nice way of doing it. Let me describe it to you."

He did so, but the Khoja said, "I cannot remember all these details. Write down the recipe on a piece of paper and I will cook the liver accordingly."

His friend wrote it down and handed it to him.

He was proceeding home deep in thought when a hawk pounced down, took the liver out of his hand, and flew off with it.

The Khoja, however, did not seem to mind, for he held out the recipe and called to the hawk, "What is the use of your doing that? You can't enjoy it, because I have got the recipe here."

TALES OF NASR-ED-DIN KHOJA

The Khoja's Mother-in-Law Drowned

SOME people came to the Khoja and told him that his mother-in-law had been washing the clothes in the river, that her foot slipped, she had fallen in, and her body had not yet been found.

The Khoja went to the spot, waded into the river, and began to search up-stream.

People on the bank called out, "What are you doing, Khoja? Who ever heard of a corpse floating up-stream. Follow the current and look for it down below."

The Khoja shook his head and said, "Ah! you don't know how perverse she was. Everything she did was upside-down. No! you let me be. I know by experience all her little ways."

The Vicious Donkey

THE Khoja took his donkey to market and handed it over to the broker for sale.

A customer came forward and, wishing to find out its age, tried to look at its teeth.

THE VICIOUS DONKEY

The donkey at once bit him on the forehead and he drew back with an oath.

Then another customer came and tried to lift its tail. He too got a kick in the shins and went off limping and swearing.

The broker now came to him, and said, "It is no use, sir. No one will buy the donkey. It bites and kicks whenever it gets a chance."

"I know," said the Khoja. "As a matter of fact I did not bring the donkey here in order to sell him, but to let all good Moslems see and understand what I have to put up with."

Can a Man bite his own Ear?

WHEN the Khoja was Cadi of Akshehir two men came into Court and one accused the other of having bitten his ear.

The other said, "No, your Honour! He bit his own ear."

The Khoja said, "Come back later on and I will give you an answer."

He then crossed over to the harem and went into his private room. "Let me see," said he, "whether it is possible for a man to bite his own ear." He caught hold of his ear and while struggling to bite it fell on his back and hurt his head. He tied it up with a rag and went back to Court.

The parties returned, and the plaintiff, wishing to traverse the claim of the defendant, said, "Your Honour! is it conceivable that a man should bite his own ear?"

"Yes, my lad," answered the Cadi, "he can! He does! Not only so, but he also falls and breaks his head."

Driving to Sivri-hissar in his Night-clothes

EARLY one morning the Khoja was told that an ox-cart was just passing the door on its way to his native town, Sivri-hissar. He at once jumped out of bed and sprang into the cart just as he was.

The Khoja was so universally respected that people overlooked his little eccentricities.

When, however, they came near to Sivri-hissar the carter sent a man ahead to tell the people that the Khoja had arrived. They all came out to meet him, but when they saw that he was half naked, they asked him the reason, and he answered, " I am so fond of you all that in my hurry to get away I quite forgot to put on my clothes "

The Greengrocer's Bill

THE Khoja was passing the greengrocer's shop when the man reminded him that he had not paid his bill.

The Khoja wanted to get out of paying, but thought he must satisfy the man somehow or other, so he said, " Show me the account. Let me see how much I owe you."

While the man was turning the pages of the account-book the Khoja looked over his shoulders.

Anyone could see that in the course of years the man had gained many hundreds of piastres by charging five times more than he should have done. At the end of the account there was an entry against the Khoja's name of thirty-one piastres.

The Khoja noticed that on the opposite page there was an entry against the Cadi's name of twenty-six piastres.

He turned to the man and said, " Look here. It seems that I owe you thirty-one piastres and the Cadi twenty-six. He and I are old friends and don't stand on ceremony with one another. Let us split the difference. Suppose we say that we each owe twenty-six. How much remains? Five! Now you give me the five, and we shall be just right."

The man seemed to be delighted that the two accounts should be settled in this way and handed the Khoja the five piastres. The Khoja then wished him good morning with a chuckle to himself; but when the man was left alone he began to puzzle over this round-about way of settling an account and could not make head or tail of it.

Ammonia as a Stimulant

ONE day the Khoja was going up the mountain when his donkey refused to budge.

Someone said "Buy some ammonia from the chemist and rub it behind. You'll soon see how he will go."

When the Khoja tried it, the donkey began to run in an agony.

AMMONIA AS A STIMULANT

As the Khoja was returning home next day he felt rather tired and listless, so he tried the same medicine on himself. The result was that he got home before the donkey, but he could not stop still and began running here and there.

His wife called out, "What is the matter with you, Khoja?"

"If you want to catch me," said he, "you will have to use some ammonia too!"

The Drunken Cadi

THERE was a Cadi at Sivri-hissar named Bekri.

One day he was lying drunk in his vineyard, his cloak on one side of him and his turban on the other.

The same day our friend the Khoja went out for a walk, accompanied by his pupil Hamed, and finding the Cadi in this condition, the Khoja took up his cloak, put it on, and walked off with it. When the Cadi woke up and missed the cloak, he called the constable and told him to keep a sharp look-out and if he found anyone with it, he was to arrest him and bring him into Court.

The constable saw the Khoja wearing it and immediately arrested him. He brought him in while the Court was sitting, and the Khoja at once began his story.

"Yesterday I went for a walk with Hamed, and we came upon a fellow lying drunk in a vineyard. He had been sick, his turban and cloak were lying about, and I took the cloak and put it on. I have witnesses and plenty of evidence to prove it. Find the owner of the cloak, and I will give it to him."

The Cadi answered, "I wonder who it could be! Some extravagant fellow, I should say, judging by the look of it; but as you have been wearing it, I don't wish to have anything more to do with it."

Young Nasr-ed-Din in Charge of the Door

ONE morning his mother said to young Nasr-ed-Din, "I am going for a walk with our neighbours to the shore of the lake," and she gave him strict injunctions to take charge of the street-door, saying, "Mind, you are not to leave it."

The boy sat down on the door-step eating

NASR-ED-DIN IN CHARGE OF THE DOOR

some dried apricots which his mother had given him. While he was there, his uncle came from the village, thinking that the boy's mother was at home.

"My lad," said he, "go and tell your mother that your aunt and I are coming this evening," and so saying he left.

Nasr-ed-Din at once took the door off its hinges, put it on his back, and went off to the shore.

His mother saw him, and called out, "My boy, whatever are you doing?"

He answered: "You told me not to leave the door, but Uncle told me to tell you that he and Aunt are coming this evening. What else could I do to please you both?"

The Khoja makes Game of the Blind Men

ONE day some blind men were sitting on a bench in front of a cafe when the Khoja passed by.

As he did so he rattled the coins in his money-bag, saying, "Here! Catch hold and divide them between you!" but as he had not given them anything he waited to see what would happen.

They began to shout, "Where is it? He gave it to you. No, he did not! I will have my rights! Give me my share!"

There was a tussle, and they rolled off the bench one on top of the other.

Then they took to their sticks and had a pitched battle, while the Khoja looked on, roaring with laughter.

The Midnight Patrol

THE Khoja was walking the streets at midnight when the Governor with his patrol came upon him and asked what he was doing there at such an hour.

"My sleep has left me," answered he. "I am trying to catch it."

The Bellows

THE Khoja lighted a fire, took the bellows to it, then stopped up the nozzle and hung it up again.

When he was asked why he put the stopper in, he answered, "To keep the air in, of course. I don't like waste."

THE HARE AND THE BARLEY-MEASURE

The Loan of a Donkey

ONE day a neighbour asked the Khoja for the loan of his donkey. "It is not here," said he.

Just at that moment the donkey began to bray.

"Hullo!" said the man, "you say it is not here, and there it is braying!"

The Khoja shook his head at him, "You are a strange fellow. You believe my donkey, but don't believe me, in spite of my grey beard!"

The Hare and the Barley-measure

WHILE cutting wood upon the hills the Khoja came upon a hare. Strange to say, he had never seen one before.

"It must be a rare animal," he said to himself; "I had better show it to a native One of them is sure to know what it is."

He put in into a bag, tied it securely, an carried it home.

He told his wife about it, and said, " B careful not to open the bag. Meantime will call in a native and show him the animal."

Of course when you are told not to do a thing you immediately want to do it, and no sooner was the Khoja's wife left alone, than she said to herself, " He is up to some mischief. Let us see what this thing is."

Directly she opened the bag the hare sprang out, made for the chimney, and escaped.

She of course got a terrible fright, and not knowing what to do under the circumstances, caught hold of the first thing she could find (a barley-measure) and put it into the bag. She tied the mouth of the bag securely and sat waiting to see what would happen.

She thought the Khoja might possibly bring in one or two wiseacres to see the animal. Perhaps, however, they would only laugh at him and refuse to come, and, if so, the affair would soon blow over.

Alas for her hopes! When the Khoja went out, he met some notables and officials who were returning from a party and happened to be passing the house.

They asked him what he was so excited

THE HARE AND THE BARLEY-MEASURE

about and made him tell them the whole story.

"What can it be?" they said. "Let us go in and have a look."

So they all crowded into the Khoja's reception-room and sat down.

The Khoja impressed upon them that they should all hold up their hands and remain perfectly silent while he brought in the bag.

This he now did, holding it with the greatest care, and as he proceeded to untie the string, the visitors looked on in the greatest excitement.

When it was emptied and the barley-measure rolled on the floor, the Khoja was so astonished that he did not know what to say. At last he blurted out the words, "Ah, yes! a barley-measure! Ten of these make one kilo."

The Omnipresent Deity

THEY asked him, "Where is God?"

"What need to ask?" said he. "Is there any place where He is not?"

TALES OF NASR-ED-DIN KHOJA

A Summary of Medical Science

ONE day the Khoja said, "The sum of medical science is this: Keep your feet warm, your head cool, be careful what you eat, and do not think too much."

He cannot tell which is his Right Side in the Dark

A MAN came to stop the night with the Khoja.

They went to bed, and at midnight the man said, "There is a candle on your right side, please give it me."

The Khoja answered, "You stupid! How can I tell which is my right side in the dark?"

The Khoja's Abyssinian Pupil Hamed

THE Khoja had a pupil named Hamed—a black from Abyssinia. One day some people asked the Khoja what were those ink-spots on his clothes?

"Yesterday," he answered, "Hamed was

late for his lesson. He came running in, all of a sweat, and as he kissed my hands some drops of perspiration fell on me."

The Changeling

THE Khoja's donkey died. His wife said to him, "We cannot do without one, so take these six piastres to the market and buy another."

The Khoja bought one, and was leading him along without giving a glance behind, when two young rascals saw him. They passed the word to one another, and quietly slipped off the halter. One of them took the donkey back to the market and sold it on their joint account, while the other put the halter on his own head and arrived with the Khoja at his front door.

When the Khoja looked back and saw a man standing in the donkey's place he was struck with amazement and said, "Hullo! What on earth are you?"

At this the boy began to snivel, turn up his eyes, and whine. "Ah, sir!" he said, "my own stupidity. I offended my mother and she was furiously angry. In her anger she cried, 'I wish this son of mine to be changed into a donkey!' and lo! I at once became a donkey.

"They took me to the market and sold me, and it was you, sir, who bought me. It is by your kind intervention that I have become a man again."

He went on to say how grateful he was; but the Khoja said, "Be off with you, and don't play the fool again."

The next day the Khoja went off again to buy a donkey. When he saw that the same one which he had bought yesterday was being taken round by the broker, he went up, stooped down and said in its ear, "Ah! You silly fool! Of course you would not listen to my advice and have made your mother angry again!"

Riddles in the Pulpit

ONE day at Akshehir the Khoja went up into the pulpit to preach.

"Oh, ye faithful!" he began, "know ye what I am going to say to you?"

"We do not know," they answered.

RIDDLES IN THE PULPIT

"Well," said the Khoja, "ignorance is bliss. It will be better that I should not tell you," and so saying he left the pulpit.

Again he went up to preach and asked the same question.

The congregation answered, "Yes! We know."

"Oh! In that case," said the Khoja, "whatever is the use of my telling you?"

They were now very much perplexed, and after talking the matter over decided that if he should ask the same question again, they would answer, "Some of us know and some of us do not know."

On the next occasion when the Khoja preached and asked the same question, that was the answer which they gave him.

The Khoja replied quite seriously, "Very well! In that case let those who do know tell those who do not know."

Change for a Pound

THE Khoja sat talking with some people when a man with whom he had a slight acquaintance came up and begged him to give him change for a pound.

The Khoja, who did not like to say before all these people that he had no money in his pocket, turned his head away saying, "Is this the time to ask such a thing when you see that I am engaged?"

The man, however, persisted, for he wanted the change badly, and the Khoja was forced to think of some way of getting out of the difficulty.

"Very well!" said he. "Give me the coin!" He began to turn it over in his hand as if he were testing its weight. At last he said, "I am sorry, my lad, but I cannot change it. It is short of weight."

"Oh, please, Khoja!" said the man. "Change it and charge me what you like for the shortage. I don't mind."

The Khoja began to mutter, "Confound you. I cannot change it. It is very light indeed!" but the man clasped him by the hand saying, "Give me what you like! Afterwards I will take the coin back to the place where I got it and give you your money in full. You will be doing me a great favour if you will."

The Khoja began to break out into a perspiration and felt very angry. Deter-

THE KHOJA HIDES IN THE PANTRY.

CHANGE FOR A POUND

mined to get rid of the fellow, after turning and tossing the coin repeatedly, he turned to him and said, " I have made the calculation. You have not only to give me the pound, but must bring me six and a half piastres besides before I can change it."

The Khoja hides in the Pantry

ONE day the Khoja's daughter went into the pantry to fetch something and came upon her father lying upon the ground, hidden behind some oil-jars.

" Whatever are you doing here, father ? " she asked.

" It is your mother, my dear. I am hiding from her. Oh! what a time I have had ! "

A Plot to Steal the Khoja's Shoes

ONE day the boys of the parish arranged to play a trick upon the Khoja.

" Let us make him climb a tree, and while he is up we will steal his shoes," they said.

Standing at the foot of a tree they began

to discuss the question in great excitement. " No one can climb that tree," they cried.

The Khoja passed by and, hearing what they said, went up to them.

" I will," said he—" I'll climb that tree ! "

" You can't," said they. " It looks very easy, but it is not every smart young fellow can do that. So you let it alone."

The Khoja became very angry. " I'll show you," said he, " whether I can do it or not," and tucking up his skirts he proceeded to squeeze his shoes into his pocket.

" Why put your shoes into your pocket ? " they asked. " You won't want them up the tree."

" How do you know I shall not ? " said he. " Let me keep them handy in case I should fall."

Travellers' Tales

THERE was a Persian who came to Akshehir and told travellers' tales about Ispahan. He said that the Shah had any number of palaces there containing from 100 to 150 rooms and each palace so many thousand yards square.

The Khoja retorted, "Oh yes, but at Broussa, which is our capital, we have plenty like them. The length of the new palace is 5,000 yards and ——"

But at that moment another Persian came in, who said that he had just come from Broussa.

The Khoja felt that he could not go on like this, so he said, "The width of the palace was fifty yards."

"That is very odd," said the first Persian; "the length and breadth should always be in proportion."

"Yes," said the Khoja, "I was going to make the width agree with the length, but that Persian gentleman there came in just at the wrong moment and spoilt it all!"

The Khoja and the Students

THE Khoja met some students in the street and invited them to go home with him. He brought them up to the street-door and saying, "Wait a moment," went in and told his wife she must manage to get rid of those young fellows who were standing before the door.

His wife, pretending that she knew nothing about them, peeped out and asked what they wanted, saying at the same time, " My husband is out."

The students answered, " But, dear lady, we came here together just now. He insisted upon our coming."

The Khoja's wife repeated that he was not at home, and the students cried out that he was.

As the dispute grew louder the Khoja became impatient and put his head out of the window.

" Gentlemen, what are you quarrelling about ? " said he. " Perhaps there are two front doors : he may have gone in by one and come out by the other."

The National Dish Helwa

ONE day he was chatting with some friends, when the conversation turned upon the national dish, helwa.

" Some years ago," said the Khoja, " I wanted to make some helwa flavoured

THE NATIONAL DISH HELWA

with almonds, but I could never manage to do it."

"That is very odd. It is not difficult at all. Why couldn't you make it?" they asked.

"Well," said he, "when there was flour in the larder there was no butter, and when there was butter there was no flour."

"Oh, nonsense, Khoja! Do you mean to say that all that time you could not find both?"

"Ah, yes," he answered, "it did happen once, but then you see I was not there to make it."

The Game of Jereet

ONE day Tamerlane invited the Khoja to take part in a game of jereet.*

The Khoja had a big stout ox in his stable, which he immediately saddled and rode it to the jereet ground.

When the people saw him, they roared with laughter.

Tamerlane sent for the Khoja and said,

* See Appendix.

"You know that for the game of jereet you ought to have a pony—an animal that is clever and can fly like a bird. What made you ride an ox—a heavy log like that?"

"It is quite true, your majesty, that it is from five to ten years since I rode him last, but I know what he was when he was a calf. He ran so fast, no horse could catch him, let alone a bird."

The Khoja and the Shepherd

ONE day the Khoja was walking up the mountain pass when he met a shepherd.

The man asked him if he were a philosopher, and the Khoja said he was.

"Look, sir," said he, "at those stupid people down in the valley yonder. I asked them a question, but they could not give me an answer. Come now! Let us agree that if you are able to answer my question I shall put it, but if you cannot answer it, I will not."

"I can. What is the question?" asked the Khoja.

The shepherd replied, "You know that the new moon is very small, that it grows larger

THE KHOJA AND THE SHEPHERD

and larger until it is the size of a cart-wheel, that from the fifteenth day of the month it begins to wane until it becomes a thin crescent and finally disappears. What do they do with that old moon?"

"Do you mean to say you don't know?" said the Khoja. "Why, they cut up the old moon into long strips to make lightning. Don't you notice when there is a storm, how it flashes like a sword?"

The shepherd said, "Bravo, philosopher, you are quite right. That is my idea also."

Buying Flutes for the Village Boys

THE Khoja was going to market, and the boys of the parish asked him to bring a flute when he came back.

To each one he gave his promise, but one of them brought him the money and said, "That is for mine."

They all waited for the Khoja's return that evening, and when he came into the town they came round him, crying, "The flutes, Khoja. Where are the flutes we asked for?"

The Khoja took out one flute and handed

it to the boy who had paid for it, saying, "Only the boy who paid for his flute may play the flute."

The Khoja as a Nightingale

THE Khoja went into a man's garden, climbed up an apricot tree and began to eat the fruit. While he was doing so the owner came and asked what business he had up that tree.

The Khoja replied, "I am a nightingale. I come here to sing!"

"Very good!" said the man, "let me hear you."

When the Khoja began, the man could not help laughing.

"Is that the way a nightingale sings?" he asked.

"Yes," said the Khoja—"a nightingale that is out of practice!"

The Khoja and the Beggar

THE Khoja was sitting at home one day when a man knocked at the street-door. He called out to him, "What do you want?"

THE KHOJA AND THE BEGGAR

"Please come down for a moment," said the man.

The Khoja went down, and when he came to the door found that it was a beggar. He felt very much annoyed, but said to the man quietly, "Come upstairs with me."

When the beggar had climbed up to the top floor where the Khoja had been sitting, the latter turned to him and said, "I have nothing for you, my man."

"Well," said the beggar, "since you meant to send me away without anything, why did you not tell me so downstairs?"

"And you, my good man, why did you not tell me what you wanted instead of making me go all the way downstairs?"

Impertinent Critics

THE Khoja was going to a village with his son. He put the boy on the donkey and walked alongside.

Some people saw them and said, "Look at these young fellows of the present day Fancy making his old father walk while ' rides the donkey in comfort!"

219

The boy heard them and said, "Father, that is not my fault; I did not insist upon it. Now, don't be obstinate, but get up."

The Khoja did so, and they had gone but a short distance when several people passed and called out: "Oh, you hard-hearted brute! Isn't it a shame to make the poor lad run like that and bake in the sun?"

The Khoja immediately pulled up, took the boy and put him up behind.

They had not gone far before a party of roughs met them and said, "What cruelty! Two people riding on one donkey and evidently come from a distance. Just see that fellow. He is a Khoja! How disgraceful!"

At last the Khoja lost his temper, and they both got down and drove the donkey on before them.

Then some others came along, and when they saw them cried, "What stupid people! Fancy letting their donkey go free and easy like that, while they trudge along in all this heat and dust and dirt. What idiots there are in the world!"

When the Khoja heard them he said,

"Oh, I would give anything to make these people hold their tongues!"

Tamerlane and the Khoja at the Bath

TAMERLANE went to the bath with the Khoja and asked him in the course of conversation, "If I had been a slave, I wonder how much I would be worth?"

"Fifty piastres," answered the Khoja.

"You blockhead," said he angrily, "the cloth round my loins is worth fifty."

"Just so," answered the Khoja coolly. "I estimated your value at the price of that rag."

The Khoja Tongue-tied

ONE day the Khoja went up into the pulpit to preach. The people crowded into the mosque and sat waiting to hear him.

He sat there for a long time, but could think of nothing, and as he saw the eyes of the people fixed upon him he became very nervous, and the more nervous he felt the more tongue-tied he became.

At last when he realized the fact that he

had nothing at all to say, he turned to the congregation and said: " Good people, you evidently know that I am quite unable to speak to-day. Indeed, I wonder if you think it was right for me to have got into the pulpit at all ? "

The Khoja's son happened to be sitting just under the pulpit, and when he heard his father say this, he got up and said, " Father ! if you cannot think of anything to say you might at least have the decency to get out of the pulpit."

In saying this he not only showed that he was indeed the son of his father, but he saved the poor man from a dilemma.

The Fish that swallowed Jonah

WHILE the fishermen were dragging their nets at the lake the Khoja stood watching them. He was so absorbed that he quite forgot where he was. His foot slipped and he fell into a net. The fishermen cried, " Why, Khoja, what have you done ? "

" Oh ! " he answered, " I am one of them. I am the fish that swallowed Jonah."

Honey for the Cadi of Konia

THERE was a Cadi at Konia who was very fond of taking bribes. The Khoja had to send to Konia to get a decree confirmed by the Court, but he was kept waiting for months, and though he tried every possible means to persuade the Cadi, he could not get him to do it. Finally he was obliged to go to Konia himself.

He took with him a large jar which he gave to the Cadi as a bribe. The latter opened it in his private room, and when he saw that it contained some very fine honey he went into the reception-room where the Khoja was waiting, treated him with the greatest cordiality, and proceeded at once to confirm the decree and hand it over to him. The Khoja put the document into his pocket and with a foxy smile on his face took leave.

A day or two afterwards another man sent a dish of cream as a present and the Cadi thought he would eat some of the honey with it. He dipped the spoon into the jar, when he saw that underneath the honey was a lot of dirt.

He was furious, called the constable, and

told him to find that rascal Nasr-ed-Din Khoja and try under some pretence to get him to come back to the Court.

The constable came upon the Khoja in the market just as he was making his preparations to return to Akshehir.

He went up and, after respectfully kissing the hem of his garment, said, " Sir, there was an error in the wording of that document. The Cadi sends his kind regards, and I am to tell you that he will correct it and give it back to you."

The Khoja gave the man a sarcastic smile, and said, " There was nothing wrong with that document, for the Clerks of the Court (God bless them) were very careful to see that it was all right; but there was certainly something very wrong with that jar ! "

So saying, the Khoja went on with his preparations and then left for home.

A Cure for the Scab

A VILLAGER had a goat which was attacked by the scab. His friends advised him to rub it with tar, but he took it first to the Khoja.

A CURE FOR THE SCAB

"I am told, sir," said he, "that your breath is an excellent cure for the scab. Would you be so kind as to breathe on my goat?"

"All right," said the Khoja, "I will breathe on it if you wish; but if you want it to get well quickly you must mix a little tar with my breath."

The Dirty Melons

ONE day the Khoja went up the mountain to cut wood and took some melons with him.

Becoming thirsty, he cut one, but finding that it had no taste, threw it away. Then he cut another, and so he went on until he had tried them all.

He ate a bit of each and threw the rest on to a muck-heap close by.

Later on he again felt hot and thirsty, and as he could not find any water to drink went back to the pieces of melon which were lying in the dirt.

"H'm! that is not so bad," said he, picking up a bit and eating it; "but that —ah! that is too dirty!"

However, he went on until he had eaten them all.

Instructions to the Donkey

THE Khoja had been cutting wood on the mountain and loaded it on his donkey. He threw the axe and his cloak on top and said, "I am going by the mountain path. You go by the high-road."

When he arrived he found that the donkey had not turned up, and said to himself, "Just think of it! I have come quicker than the donkey. What a good walker I am!"

But as time passed and no donkey arrived, he said, "I had better go and see what has become of him."

When he got up to the mountain he found the animal grazing on the very spot where he had left him, but of his cloak and the axe there was nothing to be seen. He at once threw down the wood from the donkey's back, leaving him with the saddle on.

Then he began to scold him. "Here you are feeding just where I left you. Very good! Now be off and bring back my cloak and the axe and take the saddle with you!"

THE BED-QUILT

The Khoja ill-treats his Daughter

THE Khoja handed his daughter a water-jar, and as he did so gave her two smacks in the face, saying, "Mind you don't break the jar!"

Some people who saw the innocent child beaten in this way turned to the Khoja and said, "Is it not a shame to ill-treat the poor child without a cause?"

"No!" said he, "I must show her the serious consequences of breaking the jar before she breaks it, so as to make her pay attention. It would be no good punishing her after she had broken it."

The Bed-quilt

THE poor Khoja and his wife had only one bed-quilt between them. In the winter they used to cover themselves with the Khoja's coat or anything that came to hand.

One night when there was a heavy fall of snow his wife said to him, "Khoja, you are not earning anything. We are very hard up.

We have not even an extra quilt, and you say the one we have must do. Oh! if we only had two, how comfortable we would be! I hate having to put up with anything we can get. One thing is too long and the other too short; one slips over the edge of the bed, the other gathers into a hard lump in another place. Oh, curses on such poverty! But what can we do? I remember that my father once . . ."

But when she began this the Khoja, who had for years listened to these same stories and indeed knew them now even better than she did herself, broke in, saying, "Stop grumbling, will you? I am tired and want to go to sleep, and you go to sleep too!"

But once her tongue had begun to wag it was quite impossible to stop her, so he said, "Come now. I will get you any amount of cotton and you shall make as many quilts or mattresses as you like."

So saying, he put a sack on his shoulder and went down to the yard, where he began to fill it with snow.

His wife saw him from the window and cried out, "What are you up to? You will make yourself ill playing with the snow in this hard frost, and then I shall have something else to worry about! What are you going to do with that snow?"

"There you are," said he. "Cotton! Any amount of it! Come straight from God!"

"What!" said his wife, "the idea of using snow to keep one warm!"

"Well!" said the Khoja, "if it cannot keep one warm, how is it that our fathers and grandfathers are lying under it so warm and comfortable and sleeping so peacefully?"

The Khoja's Skill with the Bow

IN the spring when the time came for the troops to go out for archery practice, Tamerlane took the Khoja with him, and in the course of conversation the Khoja happened to mention that he had at one time gone in for archery. "If so," said Tamerlane, "you must have a shot now."

The Khoja begged to be excused, but as Tamerlane insisted, he strung a bow and aimed at the target. He missed, but without a moment's hesitation said, "That was to show you how the Chief Huntsman shoots."

They then gave him another arrow and he took aim. This also went wide of the mark. "That," said he, "is the way our Governor shoots."

By a fluke the third arrow made a bull's-eye, whereupon the Khoja turned round and said with great pride, "And now you see how Nasr-ed-Din Khoja shoots!"

Payment for Attendance at the Turkish Bath

ONE day the Khoja went to the Turkish bath, but the attendants treated him with scant respect, giving him a rag for a loincloth and an old towel.

He made no remark, and when he went out left ten piastres on the hand-mirror. The attendants were very much surprised and of course delighted.

A week later he again went to the bath, when the attendants paid him the greatest attention, giving him embroidered towels and a cloth of silk.

Again he made no remark, but when he went out left only one piastre on the mirror.

The attendants were amazed and very

indignant at receiving so little, and said to him: "Khoja, is this a nice way to treat us?"

The Khoja replied, "There is really nothing extraordinary about it. The one piastre which I have given you to-day is to pay for last week's bath, and what I paid you then is for my bath to-day."

God's Guest

THERE was a big hulking loafer, a fellow without the slightest particle of shame or decency, who never went into a house without stealing something. From some houses he took clothes, from others food, and although they might beat and drive him away it had no effect, for it would not be long before he came back again.

He had constantly annoyed the Khoja in this way.

One day he was at home and the man came just when he was busy and knocked at the door.

The Khoja's wife went down and asked who was there, and he answered, "I want to see the master of the house."

The Khoja then went down and, recognising the man's voice, stood behind the door to listen. He heard the man ask his wife for food and her indignant refusal, then he himself went up to the impudent rascal and said, "What are you doing here? What do you want?"

"I am God's guest," said he.

"Ah!" said the Khoja at once. "If so, come along with me," and he took him straight to the door of the big Mosque. "You came to the wrong house, my man, if you are God's guest, for this is God's House."

Hare Soup

ONE day a villager brought a hare to the Khoja as a present, and the Khoja treated him so well that he turned up again a week later. The Khoja did not recognise him, so the man said, "I am the villager who brought you that hare last week."

The Khoja made him welcome and gave him some soup, saying, "It is soup made from the gravy of the hare. Please help yourself."

A few days later three or four villagers turned up in the hope of being entertained. He asked who they were, and they answered, "We are the neighbours of the villager who brought you that hare."

The Khoja gave them some sweets and made them welcome.

A week later a few more people came and the Khoja asked who they were. They answered, "We are the neighbours of the neighbours of that villager who brought you that hare."

"Welcome!" said he, and put a bowl of water before them.

The villagers stared at it and said, "What is it, Khoja?"

"It is," answered he, "the water of the juice of the gravy of the hare!"

The Khoja and the Trooper

THE Khoja was returning from a long journey tired, and he said to himself, "O Lord, if only I had my donkey here! At least he would lift my feet from the ground!"

As he said this, a trooper came galloping

along the road and, pointing to a young foal behind him, said to the Khoja, "Heh, gaffer! No skulking in the shade of the trees. You must work. Look you. That foal of mine is tired. Put it on your back and carry it as far as the village yonder."

The Khoja cried, "Mercy on me! It is just because I am so tired that I cannot stir."

But before he could get the words out of his mouth, the man's whip came down on his shoulders like a flash of lightning.

"Up, you rascal!" cried he. "We cannot let you people take your ease like this out in the country nor choose to say where you shall stop or when you shall move on. One says, 'What a nice place! I will sleep by the fountain and you shall lie under the pine tree,' and when you do move on like a snail you take a week to do one day's journey!"

There was no help for it! The Khoja hoisted the foal on to his back and began to run before the trooper, who every now and then made him skip as he touched him up with the whip. It took him ten minutes to reach the village, where he collapsed, falling prostrate with the foal on top of him.

The hard-hearted brute pressed him no

further, but after a little more abuse left him and went on his way.

For half an hour the wretched Khoja lay there all over blood and sweat and quite unconscious. At last he began to revive and managed to drag himself to the foot of a tree.

Then he looked up to Heaven and said, "O Lord! Evidently I was unable to explain myself properly because I had lost my teeth. What I asked for was a donkey to ride, but Thou didst send me something to ride *me!*"

The Khoja and the Vineyard

A VINEYARD at Akshehir was for sale and going very cheap. Four or five people were after it.

One of them came to the Khoja and begged him to try to get it for him, and, if possible, at a lower figure.

The Khoja at once went off to the owner and managed the business. When his client heard that it was all right, he came to him to hear what he had done.

"Oh! I managed it all right," said he,

"but I had a hard job. I laughed in the fellow's beard and had to think of all possible ways of persuading him. Then, remembering what you said to me, I tried to get it at a lower price. All this I did for your sake, and I hope you are well pleased."

The man assured him of his gratitude and began to dance for joy.

"But," continued the Khoja, "what do you say to my having done a little business on my own account?"

"What do you mean?" answered the man, "of course you will get your commission. No one can say anything against that.

"Well," said the Khoja, "after using every effort to get it cheaper as you wished me to do, I put in a word or two for myself, as I felt I had a right to be rewarded for my trouble, and so—I bought the vineyard for myself!"

The Khoja and the Sieve

THE Khoja was looking for something in the pantry when a sieve full of onions fell on his head. He got a nasty crack and for the moment was quite dazed.

THE KHOJA AND THE SIEVE

Then he said, "I'll give it such a kick!" but in doing so he barked his shins against the edge and hurt himself badly. Then in a rage he picked it up and dashed it on the ground. It rebounded and he got a cut on the forehead.

At this he rushed indoors and catching hold of a big yataghan, shouted out, "Now, I don't care how many sieves there are. Let them all come!"

The Donkey's Barley Ration

I ONCE knew a gentleman who was fond of spinning a good yarn and heard him tell this one about the Khoja.

One winter he was very hard up and said to himself "How would it do if I were to cut down the donkey's barley?"

So every time he filled the measure, he put in a little less, but the donkey remained as lively as ever; and later on, when he had reduced it by one handful, the donkey did not seem to mind.

The Khoja went on in this way until he had reduced the ration by one-half. Then it is true that the donkey became very quiet, but he looked quite fit.

Two months passed and he had reduced it to less than half. Now the poor brute was not only quiet but looked miserable. He came to that state when he could scarcely stand and rarely touched his straw. His ration of barley was just a handful.

One morning the Khoja entered the stable and found him dead.

"Ah!" said he, "just when we were getting him accustomed to it! 'Tis the will of Providence!"

The Khoja buys a Sporting Dog for the Governor

A VERY miserly Governor of Akshehir once called the Khoja and said, "I hear that you are very fond of hunting and know a lot of sportsmen. I wish you would get me a greyhound. I want one with the ears of a hare, the legs of a deer, and the girth of an ant."

Shortly afterwards the Khoja came back leading by a rope a sheep-dog as big as a donkey.

KHOJA BUYS SPORTING DOG FOR GOVERNOR

" What is this ? " asked the Governor.

" The dog. Didn't you ask me to get you a dog ? "

" Did I not tell you I wanted a greyhound, as thin and swift as a mountain goat ? "

" Oh, don't be uneasy," said the Khoja. " In your house it will not be long before it is as thin as you please."

The Donkey and the Frogs

WHILE coming home from a distant village the donkey became very thirsty, and directly it caught sight of the lake it broke away and rushed for the water. This happened at a spot where there was a sharp, precipitous descent. The poor brute was on the point of falling over when some frogs began to croak, which made him shy and jump aside. The Khoja was so delighted that as he caught hold of the donkey, he took a handful of coins out of his pocket and scattered them over the lake, crying, " Bravo, ye lake birds ! Take this and buy yourselves some sweets ! "

Loan of his Donkey

ONE day a neighbour asked him to let him have his donkey.

He answered, "I must go and ask him. If he is willing, I will let you have him."

After a while he came back. "I am sorry," he answered, "but the donkey is not willing. He said to me, 'If you give me to strangers, they will hit me on the ears, I shall bite *them*, and they will curse *you!*'"

Laying Eggs at the Turkish Bath

ONE day the boys of Akshehir took the Khoja to the Turkish bath, and each one took an egg with him without letting the Khoja know.

They all undressed, went in and sat down on the shampooing bench. Then they began to call to one another, "I say! let us lay eggs! Whoever cannot lay an egg must pay for the bath."

Then they squeezed themselves up like hens, crying, "Ghaid! Ghaid! Ghaidak!" and each one proceeded quietly to lay on the

LAYING EGGS AT THE TURKISH BATH

marble slab the egg which he had brought with him

The Khoja, seeing them do this, immediately began to wave his arms and cry, "Cock-a-doodle-do!"

The boys called out, "'What are you doing, Khoja?" and he said, "Why, where there are so many hens, surely one cock is necessary! Cock-a-doodle-do!"

"*Gloomy Fatima*"

ONE evening the Khoja returned home tired and out of sorts and longing for something to cheer him up, when he saw that his wife wore the usual scowl on her face.

"Hullo! Gloomy Fatima!" he cried, "what is wrong now? Is this my reward for toiling from morn till eve for your sake that you meet me with a face like that?"

"Ah!" said she, "and with very good reason too! A greyhound belonging to a friend of mine attacked a child and killed it. I went to see it and have just come back."

"Liar!" said the Khoja. "I happen to know that you have just come back from a wedding."

TALES OF NASR-ED-DIN KHOJA

He shoots a Figure in the Moonlight

ONE moonlight night the Khoja saw a terrible figure standing in his garden with outstretched arms. He at once woke up his wife and said, "Be quick! My bow and arrow!

When she brought it, he strung the bow to its utmost and crying "In the name of God," sped the arrow to its mark. He could see that it had struck the figure in the pit of the stomach, and said, "What a fine shot! Let the fellow stay till morning and writhe in agony." Then he came in, shut the door carefully and lay down to sleep.

Early in the morning he got up, went into the garden, and found that the figure which he had shot was his own cloak which his wife had washed the day before and hung on the clothes-line to dry. There was a big hole right through the middle. No sooner did he see this than he began to pray and to cry out, "A thousand thanks, O Lord!"

His wife asked him what was the matter and why he was giving thanks.

"Silly woman," said he, "don't you see where the arrow went in? It went right through the pit of the stomach! Think what would have become of me if I had been inside!" He kept one hand on the pit of his stomach, while from his mouth he poured forth praise and thanksgiving.

The Pleasure Party

IN the spring the Khoja went with his relations to a neighbouring village where there was plenty of running water and gardens full of fruit and vegetables of every description. It was a veritable paradise. The grass was studded with flowers in full bloom, the trees pink and white with blossom, and they enjoyed it all immensely. They beguiled the passing hour with laughter and song and did justice to the good food which they had brought with them.

At last it was time to go, but no one wished to leave the lovely spot and they decided to remain a few days. Each one promised to contribute something towards the general entertainment. One said he would bring baklawa, another stuffed lamb, another mince meat cooked in vine leaves, while others would bring cheese and fruit.

Then they looked at the Khoja wondering what he would bring.

"Oh!" said he, "let the feast go on for three months I will not stay away. May the curses of God, His Prophet, and all the angels light upon me if I do!"

The Khoja's Wife provokes a Scandal

EVERY night the Khoja's wife left him in charge of the house while she went off to gossip with the neighbours.

Some of them warned him that she was associating with disreputable women.

One night she went off after making all sorts of excuses and came back late. She knocked, but the Khoja was angry and refused to open the door, in spite of her entreaties.

"Very well!" she cried, "then I'll throw myself down the well and have done with you, once for all."

She ran off and threw a big stone down the well, while she hid herself in the shadow of the wall.

Stricken with grief, the Khoja cried, "She is mad. I must go and save her!"

THE KHOJA'S WIFE PROVOKES A SCANDAL

Now, no sooner had he opened the door and stepped outside than his wife ran in and fastened the door behind her. Then she ran upstairs and began to look out of the window where the Khoja had been sitting. He called to her to open the door, but, as she took not the slightest notice, he was obliged to eat humble pie and beg her to do so. She, however, began to shout at the top of her voice, " I have had quite enough of this! Going off every night pretending that you go to see the neighbours. A pretty story indeed! Who knows what bad women you go to see. You will break your poor wife's heart. Shame on your grey beard. You are a perfect scandal. I'll let everybody know about you. I'll teach you to go off and leave me every night like this."

Amazed at her cunning in imputing to others the very indiscretions which she herself committed, and annoyed at the curiosity of the neighbours, all the poor man could say was, " Ah! I only hope that those who know the truth will publish it abroad."

TALES OF NASR-ED-DIN KHOJA

Carrying Fowls to Sivri-hissar

ONE day the Khoja packed his fowls into a cage and was taking them along the road from Akshehir to Sivri-hissar.

"Ah! the poor things! They will be stifled in this heat," said he, "I must let them out for a run."

When he did so they began to go off in every direction, so he took a stick and, putting the cock in front, began to drive them along.

"You stupid bird!" said he to the cock. "How is it that at midnight you know the approach of dawn and yet you cannot tell the road from Akshehir to Sivri-hissar!"

Ruse to obtain an Invitation to a Wedding

THE Khoja heard that a wedding was going on at a certain house. When he thought that the guests would be just sitting down to breakfast, he took a sheet of paper, folded and put it into an envelope. He then knocked at the door, and when the servant asked him what he wanted, said, "A letter for the master of the house. Urgent."

The servant let him in and, handing the letter to the gentleman, he sat down to table and began to eat.

"There is no address on the envelope," said the host.

"Oh, never mind that," said the Khoja. "The man was in such a hurry that he hadn't even time to write anything inside."

Villagers complain of the Khoja to the Cadi

THE people of the Khoja's village made a complaint against him to the Cadi about something or other, and the Cadi sent for him.

"The villagers don't want you," said he; "you must go and shift for yourself."

"Indeed!" said the Khoja. "It is I who do not want the villagers. Let them go to Hell for all I care. They are so many that wherever they go they can make a village, but how am I at my time of life to move my things without a moment's notice? Where is the mountain-top on which I can make myself a home?"

TALES OF NASR-ED-DIN KHOJA

Young Nasr-ed-Din steals the Miser's Goose

WHEN the Khoja was a boy he was always up to mischief. One day as he was going along the road he noticed in the shadow of the wall a lot of geese belonging to a neighbour who was the biggest miser and surliest brute in the parish.

Seeing that they were all asleep, he thought it a good opportunity to make the old man furious and draw a crowd about him, so he quietly caught hold of the biggest gander, slipped it under his coat and walked off with it.

He had gone some distance and was surprised to see that it remained perfectly quiet, so when he came to a street where there was nobody passing, he gently opened his coat and took a peep.

The goose at once lifted his head and hissed out " hush ! "

" Bravo, goose ! " cried the Khoja—" that is just what I was going to tell you to do. What fools people are to call you a goose ! You have far more sense than your master."

THE KHOJA ARRESTED FOR CARRYING ARMS

The Boys paddling in the River

SOME boys sat on the river-bank with their legs in the water.

"Where is my foot?" cried one. "That is not it. That is Hussein's foot. Oh, dear! our feet have all got mixed up. I told you it would never do to crowd together with our feet in the water. How on earth is each one to find his own foot?"

While they were wrangling about it, the Khoja came along, and when he heard what all the noise was about, he said, "Wait a moment. I'll soon make each of you get back his own foot, and punish the boy who got you all mixed up."

So saying, he shoved his stick into the water. When they felt it touch their legs, they all cried out in a fright. Out came their legs like magic and each one found his own.

The Khoja arrested for carrying Arms

WHEN the Khoja was a student it was strictly prohibited to carry arms of any kind.

One day he was seen walking to school

with a big yataghan stuck in his belt. He was arrested and brought before the Governor, who demanded angrily if he had not seen the notice prohibiting the carrying of arms. "What do you mean, then, by carrying about that knife in broad daylight?"

"I use it at school," he answered, "to scratch out the errors in my lesson-book."

"Ridiculous!" said the Governor. "What! use a big thing like that for such a purpose!"

"Well," said he, "sometimes the errors are so great that this is really not big enough."

The Roast Chicken

THE Khoja sat under a tree eating some roast chicken.

A man came up to him and said, "How nice! I should like some of that. Please give me a bit."

"I am very sorry, brother," answered the Khoja. "It isn't mine. It is my wife's chicken."

"But you are eating it," said the man.

"Of course," said the Khoja. "What else can I do? When she gave it to me she said, 'Eat it.'"

THE KHOJA'S LAST INSTRUCTIONS TO WIFE

Where to stand when carrying the Coffin

THEY asked the Khoja which was the best place to take when helping to carry a dead man to the cemetery.*

"Would it be better in front of the coffin, or behind?"

"So long as you are not inside yourself, it doesn't matter which," said he.

The Khoja's Last Instructions to his Wife

WHEN the Khoja was on his death-bed he called his wife and said, "My dear, I want you to put on your very best clothes, do your hair nicely, and put some colour on your face. Try to make yourself as smart as possible and then let me see you."

"My dear," said she, "how can I leave you at such a painful moment? How can I think of dressing up like that? It is im-

* *Carrying the coffin.* Four from among the near relatives carry the bier upon their shoulders, being every now and then relieved by others. One bier is used for all and is kept at the Mosque. The dead are buried without a coffin.

possible. I would not do it for the world. And why is it necessary? Can you think me so heartless, so ungrateful?"

"No, little wife," said he. "These are things you cannot understand. I was thinking of something very different. I see that my end is at hand. Azrail,* the Angel of Death, is hovering near. I thought that perhaps if he saw you in these fine clothes looking like an angel or a peacock, he might take you and leave me. That is what I wanted. Now do you understand the meaning of it?"

The poor woman stared at him aghast not knowing what to say or what to do. Then one of the old women who were in the room said, "God forgive you, Khoja, but you cannot stop joking even at the point of death."

The Apparition

ONE Friday morning long after the Khoja's death a crowd of people had assembled for midday service at the old Mosque in Akshehir, when suddenly a figure

* *Azrail.* The Angel of Death.

THE APPARITION

appeared at the main entrance looking exactly like him with the same smiling face and familiar, quaint costume.

"Good people," he cried, "I have such a strange thing to tell you. I had just performed my ablutions and was going to lock the door of my grave when whom do you think I saw? Nasr-ed-Din Khoja!! There he was as large as life. It was his face with the same comical expression and he was wearing those funny clothes of his. He was sitting astride on his coffin, looking about him, and he said to me, 'Go and tell the people at the big Mosque to come and see me. If anyone fails to come, it will be at his peril.'"

The people, who had implicit faith in the Khoja and were also favourably impressed by his messenger, rushed to the grave, but of course they saw no Khoja there.

So they came away laughing as they remembered how often they had heard their fathers and grandfathers tell them of similar tricks they had seen him play.

"You naughty Khoja," they cried, "you cannot resist the temptation to come out every now and then and have a game. It is your little way of letting us know that you are always with us."

They then all joined in repeating the "*Fatihat*" * and returned to the Mosque, but when they arrived they found that, while they were away, the dome had disappeared.

* The opening sentences of the Koran. It is as sacred an utterance to a Mohammedan as the Lord's Prayer is to a Christian.